NO
BONDS
SO
STRONG

NO BONDS SO STRONG

Tarik D. Daniels

MisterTellTales

"There are no bonds so strong as those which are formed by suffering together"

-Harriet Ann Jacobs

Dear AfroQueer,

I write this letter to you with a heavy heart about the fear that runs deep in all of us who are black and queer in America. As black people, we are bonded through hundreds of years of colonization on the continent of Africa, and the systematic oppression of slavery in America. We are rooted in the Jim Crow Laws of the South, as well as the segregation of our blackness from the Anglo whiteness. We are black. We are afro. Somewhere along the lines, our queerness removed us from the bond that has been running through our bloods for centuries; that same bond that has been passed down through generations into a new place of double oppression. Our own people have turned their backs on us. The cisgender black man and black woman have declared war on the Afro-Queer.

Somewhere along this journey, being queer has become a burden in the fight of justice among our people, even though queerness has always been at the front lines of every major fight for justice and equality. Somewhere along our path, it became okay for our black brothers and sisters to look down on us and treat us as as though we were sub-human because of our queerness. The war has been very loud with homophobic behaviors and teachings against us, and the war has been very silent as our former allies refused to speak out against these homophobic behaviors and teachings. The blood is on their hands because they have allowed the mistreatment and murders of our black transgendered sisters and brothers, all while they remained silent.

This betrayal from our former allies of the brother and sisterhood has affected our afro-queer youth the worst. It has been their enforcement of heteronormative upbringing into our afro-queer youth, and horrible biblical teachings, that has traumatized our children. This continues to lead to a rise in suicide attempts, and it aides in the devaluation of their lives. In our community we have been called "faggots" by black people way before we were ever called "niggers" by white people. So, I ask the question, who is the real enemy?

We cannot continue to support these black liberation movements in our country until we are represented, and done so very unapologetically. Spaces have to be created to allow our wants and needs to respectfully have a seat at the table. The table where we need to be, is one that we should have never been forced to leave from. The black church has always been a site of great social and spiritual importance for black people in our fight against racial oppression, but now a bible that was used to enslave us is being used to betray us, for this I blame the miscommunications of the purpose of the church. It's their duty to protect us, and abolish this negative religious rhetoric within our community and family structures.

I ask that we take a stand, and not continue to fall victim to this reverse homophobia agenda from black liberation movements who seek to attack whiteness within the LGBTQ community, but doesn't show praise towards blackness within that same community. It's nothing more than a distraction from the real truth. Demand change in your communities, and with your family and friends. Use the few allies we have to let cisgender black people across the nation know enough is enough! It's not about being radical, it's about right! Due to our intersectionality of race, religious, and sexual identities, we must seek justice and equality in all facets of our lives. We are Black! We are Queer! We are Afro-Queer!

MisterTellTales

Table of Contents

Trayvon 1
Eman 8
Jay Jay 13
Robert 17
Trayvon 22
Eman 27
Robert 32
Jay Jay 35
Eman 40
Trayvon 44
Robert 52
Trayvon 57
Jay Jay 63
Trayvon 68
Eman 71
Robert 77
Trayvon 82
Robert 87
Jay Jay 91
Trayvon 95
Eman 99
Robert 103
Trayvon 108
Jay Jay 113
Eman 118
Robert 123
Trayvon 126
Eman 132
Robert 137
Jay Jay 140
Trayvon 146
Jay Jay 150
Eman 154
Trayvon 159

Trayvon

Days like this, I really wish I had gone shopping earlier because I am not finding anything to wear! I mean, I need a new coat, some new boots, and a new hat because I know these Detroit girls are tired of seeing me in these same old outfits. Hell, I'm tired of wearing them. I can't even think of the last time my ass has seen a mall, let alone been in one. My great-grandma is probably not going to invest in another pair of boots anytime soon, especially since I was just robbed at gun point for my last pair of Timberlands. Damn! I still can't believe they pulled a gun out on me!

That experience was just so damn horrible. Can you imagine walking miles and miles back home with no shoes on, in six feet of snow? Ugh! My ass had to go the hospital that night because my feet were so frost bitten. And to top it off, I went to Henry Ford Hospital, and you know they call that the "death hospital." Thank God I'm still here!

My great-grandma always told me flashy stuff brings unnecessary attention in these streets. Come to think of it, she has a lot of nerves, considering her closet has at least four or five mink coats in it. Must be nice! Luckily, she doesn't spend nearly as much time as I do going out.

"Trayvon, come here," yells my great grandmother from the other room.

"Yes," I replied.

"Look at this! I told y'all to be careful going to those clubs," she says as I enter her room while she's in her bed watching the 11 o'clock news.

Now my great grandmother, aka Ge- Ge, is always watching the news. She wakes up at five o'clock in the morning to watch the first showing of the news until it goes off at nine, right before Regis and Kathie Lee comes on. Then, she starts reading the newspaper throughout the day, and then she tunes into the midday news at eleven. Afterwards, she runs her errands, and makes sure she gets back home to catch the five o' clock news until six. And then, she finishes the night with the evening news at 11. How much news can you watch in one day? It's Detroit, and a lot is always going on, but damn!

Fox 2 News Reporter:

"We have shocking new coverage about one of the biggest nightclub busts in recent history. Yesterday evening, Detroit Police responded to a tip about a nightclub off Gratiot Avenue that was operating under explicit and illegal activity. After raiding the illegally operated nightclub, it was discovered that it was an undercover homosexual prostitution ring, as well as a haven for several illegal drugs. Over 100 guns were seized from the property. Several people were arrested, while others were ticketed for criminal trespassing. This was just one of the acts our mayor, Kwame Kilpatrick, promised to clean up the streets. Many protestors believe it's just another attack from the mayor against the LBGT community"

"I already knew about this," I said as I scrolled through my text messages.

"Well it would've been nice to tell me about it. I know you probably hang out there with all those gays. I don't understand why y'all hang out so late all the time."

"I mean, I do go there sometimes. I really liked that club. They played the best music, but I wasn't there that night. Oh, but Emmanuel was there, and he got a ticket for criminal trespassing".

"Oh Lord, that boy ain't got no job, so who is paying for that?"

"Probably his momma, GeGe!"

"Well just know I ain't got no money to bail nobody outta jail! Y'all must think I am a bank or something. I'm living off my social security!"

"I know how much money you get GeGe, I deposit your check in the bank every month, remember?"

"By the way, where is my debit card anyway?"

"It's on the dining room table."

"Please put in back in my purse. When I need it, I don't want to have to look for it."

"I'll put it back on the way out."

"I got to get up early and head to the center."

"Good to know, I'm about to leave."

"Where are you going this late? Don't you have school in the morning?" She asked.

"Yes, I do."

"You should be heading to that bed of yours, then."

"I won't be out all night. I'll be back by two."

"You gone give me a heart attack, having to worry about you all night. It's dangerous!"

"I'll be fine."

"Yeah, that's what everybody says until something bad happens. I lost a son from hanging out in those streets."

"I understand, and I'll try to stay safe."

"You act just like your momma, hanging out all night."

"Love you, too, GeGe."

"Make sure you lock that door behind you, and don't forget your keys."

"Yes, ma'am," I yell back as I walk out the front door to start out my Wednesday night by leaving the lobby of the Tulip Heights.

Tulip Heights is the name of my great grandmother's senior citizen living community, and it has been my home for the last couple of years. After several arguments with my momma, stepfather, and my grandmother, GeGe's apartment has become my solace. She took me in with open arms, and never judged me for who I am. I feel safe at Tulip Heights, and it's been a while since I felt like that. I have stability, and these old folks around here are like my family. All my friends think of GeGe as their grandmother, especially Robert, who always comes to pick me up for a ride. They like how blunt she is when she talks to them. They think it's funny.

Tonight, as I got into my friend Robert's car, I looked at him and realize how distant we've become. I met him almost two years ago, and we been tight as glue since then. When we first met, I think he liked me, but he was 10 years older than me, plus size, and I was not interested at all. Not being rude or anything, but it just wasn't my thing. I just prefer to talk to guys around my age, those who are still in high school.

So, we just grew as friends, and he continued to introduce me to new people. Nowadays, I feel like I'm closer to them than to Robert, because he's just really messy. He lies, starts drama, and has lots of insecurity issues that I just can't deal with! But hey, he's still a cool friend, and a free ride (because I don't have my license yet).

"Hey honey," says Robert from the driver's seat.

"What's poppin'?" I responded.

"Grab the bottle of Bacardi out the trunk, so you can make a cocktail," he says as he pops the trunk.

"Yes, bitch, I need a drink badly."

"Girl, catch up! I'm full boots."

We all know drinking and driving is a big no no, but for us, it is an everyday thing. We have avoided spending big bucks on buying out the bar, and the fact that I'm only 16 and have a fake ID saying that I'm 18, means it would be hard for me to buy a drink. So, we buy half gallons of liquor, which is usually Bacardi Light Rum, and we buy cups, ice, and chasers. We make our drinks in the car, and we are usually drunk as skunks before we even make it to the bar. We all have a different opinion on what we like as a mixer for our cocktails, but I'm an orange juice man myself. Robert likes pineapple juice. Jay Jay and Eman both likes fruity shit.

"Oh my God! It's been a while since I've seen you, girl! I hear you been hanging out with Emmanuel and Jay Jay without me. They ya new girlfriends now?"

"Don't be dramatic, you know you still my road dog. They just started picking me up when you been so busy with your new man. We been trying to get all us linked up together for the last two weeks."

"True dat, I have been quite busy. My new man is 10 inches thick, and he keeps me quite occupied. No time to be running to Off Broadway East with y'all late girls."

"Girl, I doubt you know what to do with that anyway, so tell him when he done playing around, let him know a real nigga over here is ready," I laughed out.

"Anyway, OMG, I know you heard about what happened at the prop house the other night, right?"

"Yeah, I did. I was going to go out that night, but I had to wake up early for a final, so I told Emmanuel and Jay Jay to go without me. I'm so glad I didn't go."

"Me, too. My life would have been over if I'd gotten my mother's car impounded.

"I bet."

"You heard that new vogueing beat about Janet Jackson getting caught stealing on an episode of Good Times?"

"Of course! Everybody keeps playing it! You know I don't listen to the beats like that, though!"

"That's because you ain't got any rhythm, girl," he says as he blasts the radio really loud as we turn into the parking lot of the club.

"Oh, I got rhythm. Ask ya nigga."

"Bitch, please," Robert says as we both start laughing loud as hell.

"This street is so raggedy."

"All these fuckin' potholes!"

"Bitch, I just had to get new tires from a blowout on Outer Drive".

"I thought this new young mayor was going to fix these bad roads, and tear down all these damn abandoned buildings!"

"Girl, his black ass can't fix anything because he's too busy trying to close all the gay clubs."

"He needs to bring his gay, homophobic ass out the closet."

Club Off Broadway East is a tiny club right off the freeway on the east-side. It's really just a neighborhood pub with strippers and drag shows for entertainment, and it's small as hell. It's divided into two parts. The first part is the entrance area that also has the bar and some tables. It's almost like the lounge area where you can talk and drink. And then, you have the second room which is just an open space with a pole, and big ass mirrors on the wall.

They keep this room very dark, and all you can really see is the big ass speakers placed in each corner of the room, and a small elevated platform where people perform. The rest of the room is meant to be the dance floor. Robert really loves that club. My guess was because it was a mixed, older crowd, and maybe he connected more since he was the oldest.

This particular night at the club, I wasn't really having the best time. For one, we got there early so we could watch the drag shows, which I wasn't interested in watching. Over the past year, I have grown fond of drag and fem queens, but still not entertained with watching them lip-sync a song they barely know the words to.

I immediately find a seat on a speaker in the far corner of the tiny club, listen to Beyoncè's song, "Crazy In Love," blast out, and proceed to watch this 5'11 man dressed in the most elegant gown ever made. He (or she) is wearing this dry, dusty wig with bright red lipstick. People are steadily going to the stage throwing dollars as she, or he, is performing, which is a normal practice in the pageant scene.

Of course, Robert is the main one throwing his coins on the stage. I can bet a million dollars he will say he's broke when it's all said and done. I'm so over it! I'd much rather go to a ball with the queens, and hit the runway. I mean, I am one of the hottest new runway walkers in the ballroom scene. I also think because Emmanuel is not here, I can't let loose like I normally would.

This past year we've been having a blast because we understand each other, and have the most in common between the four of us. We all are usually together, but the bond with Eman is the closest. Don't get me wrong, Robert is fun, but tonight is just not one of those nights, and I like it better when we are all together.

After the drag show, the club went straight into a mini ball set, and of course, I battled a few people for a plaque and free drinks. The competition is not as fierce on weekdays at the club, so it was an easy win. I battled a few other girls who were new to the ballroom scene and wanted to get some exposure, but the closer it got to two o'clock in the morning, the more I was ready to go. I had school in the morning, and I had to ride three buses to get there. Plus, I was so excited that I only had a few more weeks until spring break.

"Wassup with you? You a chocolate sweet thang. How old are ya?" This older black man asks walking up to me smelling like Hennessey and Newports.

"I'm 16, papersack brown, not chocolate, and my name is Tray."

"You chocolate nigga, and you six feet, too! I like them tall, let me hold them digits."

"I'm only 5'11, and how about I don't give you my number, and you leave me hell alone!"

So, right then, I knew it was time to go.

Eman

I swear this month is just not my month. Not only did I get a ticket for criminal trespassing for being at a punk bar, I also lost my job at Target because of my attendance. I tried to get there on time every day, but my car just wouldn't act right. It's my fault for wasting my income tax check and being forced to buy this raggedy car in the first place.

I got graduation in a few weeks, and no money for my senior events. I guess I can post an ad on backpage to make some money. I took my ad down a few weeks ago after people kept getting robbed and stabbed whenever they met up with their clients. Detroit is a dangerous city, and the underground world of prostitution is even worse.

Everyday when you turn on the news, you hear of a missing Trans woman found brutally murdered, or a random gay guy found dead in a hotel room. It doesn't take a rocket scientist to figure out what went wrong in those situations. More than likely, a guy who is living a down-low lifestyle either freaks out from being exposed, or maybe he's just fucked up in the head and goes Norman Bates on their asses.

I'm not normally even a 9-5 type of guy. I believe in using my body to get what I want, which is usually not even that much. God blessed me with a cute face, nice body, phat ass, and a big dick, so why not put it to use. I'm either stripping, or escorting to make my coins.. and no, I don't do porn. It's just not my thing. I think I just live for the moment, and porn is just too permanent. It lives forever, and I don't know what my future looks like. I don't want to have footage of me fucking in cyberspace for the rest of my life.

"Jay Jay, have you talked to Trayvon today?" I asked with a fork full of lasagna.

"Yeah, I called him and told him I was cooking and y'all was coming over to watch Charmed with me. Robert is supposed to be picking him up after he takes his date home," Jay Jay replies.

"What date?"

"You know that feminine boy he been talking to for a while"

"The big dick bottom?"

"Yeah, him. That's a cute little boy."

"Yeah he is, I had sex with him about a month ago."

"Come on Emmanuel, don't tell me you had sex with Robert's date while they're together."

"I didn't know they were together"

"Doesn't matter, you knew they were talking at least. Damn! Do you have to have sex with everybody?"

"Maybe."

"Does Robert even know?"

"I don't know. If he does, then it wasn't from me. What's the big deal, anyway? It's not like they will be together long anyway. Nobody has to know shit! That boy is a jump off! He was constantly hitting my page up."

"Well, I don't wanna be involved in it when it hits the fan. Does Trayon know what happened?"

"Of course, I tell him everything. I called him the moment the jump off snuck out of my house when he heard my momma came home"

"Well, I feel like I'm forced to tell him so he don't stay looking like a fool when he's around us. And y'all wonder why he's so damn messy!"

"I didn't do it purposely, it just happened."

"So, he just happened to end up at your house, in your bed, and having sex?"

"Yup!"

"Chile. You are too much for me!"

"Okay, Piper calm down," I laugh out.

"You gotta do better Phoebe."

The television series Charmed is one of our favorite shows, and we named each other after the characters of the show. Prue is the oldest, so that's Robert. Piper is next so that's Jay Jay. I am next in age, so I'm Phoebe, which is my favorite character anyway. The youngest is Paige who replaced Prue after she died, so that's Trayvon, since he's the newest one to the circle.

All of us are pretty close at this point, even though I might be closer to Trayvon because he's like the little brother I never had. He is so innocent at times, which makes his personality so likable. He hasn't been mentally tarnished by this gay bullshit. I'm the only child, so my friends have always been my rocks. I have known Jay Jay the longest and he and Robert went to high school together back in the day.

Of course, throughout the time we have been friends, we have beefed out and not spoken several times. Robert and I have bumped heads the most, leaving Jay Jay always being the mediator. We have a love for one another that usually stands strong against our issues. Truth be told, I knew the jump off first and I introduced him to Robert. I even told him I thought the boy was cute. Robert actually went behind my back on the internet and hooked up with him just to be spiteful. Jealously is a deadly weapon, even amongst friends. And Jay Jay wants me to have remorse for hooking up with that boy. Please! In fact, fuck their relationship! Fuck all relationships.

Among our friendship, I'm often called the hot-head, or the loose cannon of the group. I'm the most masculine one who doesn't take any shit! I'm always the first one to curse a nigga out, or the first one to hit a smart mouth sissy in the club. Yes, I'm gay and all, but I'm also from the east-side of Detroit, and I don't take any disrespect! I will beat a motherfucker's ass if there is any kind of problem. These days, I try to be a lover and not a fighter, though. Fighting ain't making me no money.

Lately, I've really hated to meet up with guys from the internet at their place, but it's not like I have much of a choice since my mom caught me in the house with the Mexican dude that was paying a good penny to be my sugar daddy. He was stupid enough to leave his shoes in the living room. Once my mom got off the late-shift and saw his shoes, she busted my door down with the quickness! I really felt bad because I never wanted her to see me in that light. She has known I was gay for two years, but with her issues right now I hate for her to worry about me.

My mom has been battling cancer, and it's destroying her, but she's a warrior. Now, I just try to keep my personal life out away from her, and graduate with no problems for either of us. That is why I have to do what I have to do. I don't have a job any-more, and I got bills, so I gotta get this money the best way I can. If sharing my body will do it, so be it. Hell, I'm single, so why not!

This older dude hit my backpage account up saying he will give me $300 for an out call, which is what I need for my cap and gown payment. So, I agreed to meet up. I keep deleting my back-page account and reactivating it because I'm scared someone would expose me for having an escort account and release all of my freaky pictures. I've been hearing that's been going on lately, and I really can't deal with that kind of drama.

Luckily, this dude lives a few blocks up the street from 7 Mile, because it's hot as hell out here and I didn't wear any undies to give him easy access.

"Whats up my dude?" I ask as I gain entrance into his small apartment.

"Hey sexy, how are you?"

"I'm good, bro."

"Man, you look better in person than in your pictures! You are gorgeous! What you mixed with?"

"I'm Puerto Rican and black."

"Take a seat. Would you like a drink? I got Vodka."

"Naw, I'm good. Is it okay if I smoke a blunt?"

"Sure, I didn't know you smoked. I would have had a blunt rolled up for you already."

"You good, bro. I always keep one on me. It helps me get in the mood."

"Oh, wow! So, that's what keeps that big dick going, huh?"

"Yessir, you know it!"

"You a top?"

"Yeah, mainly. What about you?"

"I am a power bottom."

"What the fuck is a power bottom?"

"I can take your dick all night if I wanted to without any problems."

"I doubt that you can take my big dick all night," I said starting to laugh loudly.

"Well pull it out, and let me see it."

"Cool bro, but let me see that three hundred dollars, first."

"Aiight, I gotcha! It's sitting right here on the table next to the condoms."

"Cool, well come on let me feel them lips! And if you trying to go all night, that's an extra fee 'cause I got shit to do to-day."

JAY JAY

My mother can really be a thorn in my side sometimes. She always gotta have something to say about what I'm doing, and whom I'm hanging out with. I would never imagine, that at twenty-three years old, I would be still living under her roof. She thinks she can cook better than me, but she can't. I'm like Paula Deen, while she is more like Rachel Ray.

She also thinks she can dress as well as I do, but she can't. She even had the nerve to say that her hair was as long as mine. I am like, "Get real! My hair is down to my butt." She just can't face the fact that I'm just as fierce as she is. I don't know why she thinks it's a competition because it's not. I beat my mug and pad these hips and walk out in the streets and most people think I'm a girl.

It's always been like a catch twenty-two for me because I don't mind people thinking I'm a girl, but I'm still a man, and I like to be treated as such. I guess it's wanting the best of both worlds, which is well within my rights! I'm James most of the time to my family. James is dark skin, boyish looking with braids, but to my friends, I'm Jazmine.

When I get in drag, and go to clubs with my covergirl face and long black hair, I just do what I do. And I know I'm not the prettiest looking one out here, but when I get in drag, I am as real as rain. Now, don't judge me based on the relationship I have with my mother because outside of that, I'm a very nice person. Everybody considers me to be the glue of our friendship since I have never argued, or fought anyone in our crew, and I'm always there to help everybody with their issues.

My mom and I are just too close. She raised me like I was her husband since there ain't been a man in the house since I was like five. I'm starting to think she is lesbian, but who cares? I sure don't! Anyway, her bitterness is what helps me be the person I am. I strive to be the opposite of her, and I have to nurture and support people. That's something she has never been able to do.

I love spending my nights watching old movies, and I swear Mahogany has to be my favorite movie of all time! The glamour and fashion in the movie really made me want to be a fashion designer. I wanted to be male version of Mahogany, her looks and all. I simply just worship Miss Diana Ross! You can't speak about the evolution of modern-day red carpet style, or being a leading lady, without mentioning the boss, Diana Ross.

She is the undisputed fashion mother of Detroit, and a bona fide pop star. She single-handily transformed the fashion landscape with her love for luxury, and unadulterated glamour. Just like me, Diana had a passionate love for fashion and beauty. She studied modeling and cosmetology as a child, and even had dreams of becoming a fashion designer, just like I did.

Unfortunately, I dropped out of fashion school a few years ago, and I've been living in my mother's basement ever since. And I ain't designed, or styled a damn thing! I have to want more for myself than this, but the drive isn't there. Something is holding me back, and I haven't figured it out yet. The motivation is lacking, but that's all going to change next year. I'm moving to Atlanta, and I'm going to go to the Atlanta School of Design, but that's next year. For now, I just got my CDL license, and I'm going to drive trucks to get out of this city, and away from my mother. Yes, me and my long hair is driving semi-trucks! Yes Gawd!!!

"So, what are we wearing to this ball? What's the theme?" I ask Trayvon over the telephone."

"I'm thinking about all of us wearing Dickie overalls, and maybe we could personalize them to our own style," Trayvon replies.

"Dickies! Are you kidding me? That's not cunt at all, and kinda late if you ask me!"

"We already did the airbrush hoodie! Look at the last ball! Bitch, do you have any better ideas? You always talking about something being cunt."

"Not really. Well, we need to go shopping soon because I don't want to wait until the last minute to get my effect. The vogue category is asking for a lot. They want you to bring it like your favorite character from X-Men. You already know I'm going to hit the floor as Storm," I add sipping on my glass of Vodka and cranberry.

"I know, I have to walk the runway in a haute couture look with all green. I need a drink to even start thinking about what look imma give."

"Girl, I'm already over here feeling good with my cocktail and an ecstasy pill."

"Omg! Why are you taking a pill in the middle of week? You have been taking a lot of those lately."

"I'm over here having a vogue session by myself. I've been practicing for this ball, plus, I had an extra one from the club this weekend."

"That's still too much Jay Jay! Girl, you giving me addict teas!"

"Girl, you don't say anything when you are rolling from here to Africa."

"That's only on the weekends."

"Well, I need the drugs to keep the peace with all y'all drama."

"What you mean? I ain't got no drama!"

"Girl, you know I heard Eman told you about Robert's date. I didn't want to bring it up to start anything when y'all was over last week."

"Bitch, yes! He did tell me about the boy. I was like, 'Damn Eman, can you keep your dick in your pants?' "

"Girl, that's what I said. You already know this is going to blow up, so be prepared to take sides."

"Well, I told Eman he was wrong. Even if he knew him first, Robert has been very vocal about the ugly little girl."

"Why she gotta be ugly? You just saying that because she fucked Eman!"

"Girl bye! I am not checking for Eman like that! What he does is his business."

"Who are you trying to convince, Paige. Everybody already knows. You just ain't found out about your love for him. Pussy-popping sisters!"

"Whatever! We're only friends, but anyways, I got school in the morning, so I'll talk to you later."

"Holla Trayvon. I'll talk to your ass tomorrow, and make sure you get to school on time, cunt!"

I would have never imagined I would be in a circle of friends. Being the only child, I thought I was too selfish to be a good friend to different people at the same time. After several circle of friends over the years, these girls are definitely the crew I thought I would never have because we balance each other out. Well, I guess you can say I balance us all out because I'm always the level-headed one.

Trayvon is a lot like me. We never take things too seriously, and usually we can get with the flow. Even though he is only sixteen, he is pretty mature for his age. I used to call him my niece when I first meet him because of his age, but he just grew to become my sister. Now, Emmanuel and Robert are the exact opposite of us, but a lot alike because they seem to let their emotions get the best of them.

Eman is just so hot-tempered. It must be that Latino blood running through his veins. It took almost two years to get the boy to stop fighting every time we went to the club. That's my baby though! Sweetheart, but crazy. Robert is my bestie, but he is emotionally draining most times. I wouldn't trade him for the world, though. We are just four black, queer, bitches trying to make it! Where we live ain't no joke. Detroit is the place where you can get chewed up, and spit back out if you aren't careful. Luckily, I got some bitches to ride with.

ROBERT

I swear I'm going to get this triple bypass surgery and lose some of this weight. I'm just too damn big! Being a big dude in the gay scene is like death. You have to do so much more to compete with these skinny bitches. You gotta make sure your line up stays crisp. I always keep a low fade with an edge up, and a thin beard. I also have to make sure I stay fly in the latest gear, and I gotta take plenty of showers to make sure I smell good. You know they say big boys be stinky, but not my big ass!

I always smell good for the boys, and I buy the most expensive colognes. I have a glove compartment full of colognes, and I buy a new outfit every weekend! They can call me fat all day long, but one thing they can't say is I'm broke. I keep a good coin, and I don't mind spending it on some good dick. I will work overtime at the airport to pay a nigga's rent if I have to. I don't mind, shit, just as long as I'm getting dicked down. And no, I'm not an escort like Eman's trifling ass.

Anyway, I know guys typically don't go for plus size girls for free, and I don't mind, but as soon as I lose this weight... Emmanuel is going to eat his words! I just recently found out that he and my little dude had been messing around behind my back. It seems like every guy I introduce to him wants to screw Eman. I hate it, hate it, hate it! Why can't that be me? Why can't I get all the boys chasing after me? Instead, they always want my friend. If it's not Emmanuel, then it's Travyon. That's why when I do meet a boy; I keep them to myself, so I don't have to worry about losing them.

I might be fat, but I am good looking. I am light-skinned, have pretty pink lips, perfect teeth, and the cheek bones of a goddess. None of that is comparable to Eman's pretty Latino ass, and Trayvon's Taye Diggs looking-ass. Regardless, Eman knew I was dating this boy, and he fucked him anyway. I just don't understand how you can call yourself a friend, and then go and do something like that. You don't have to have sex with every cute person you meet. Damn! When I confront him tonight, it won't be cute. I'm tired of being walked all over in this group! It might be time I switched my crew up!

"I love our look tonight. I told you Jay Jay, this would be a cute outfit to put together," Trayvon said as we entered the high school gym for the biggest ball of the year.

"Well, once I put my rhinestones and glitter on my Dickies, and I painted my face like Naomi Campbell, I'm feeling it," Jay Jay added.

"Why do these balls always cost $30 dollars? I just don't get it. We are paying to go to a public high school gym, full of tables with cheap wine and potatoes chips. It's ridiculous," I complained.

"Chile, you knew how much it was before you got here, so please be quiet and let's have a good time. Let's go get that empty table in the back so I can make a drink," says Trayvon.

"Whatever! Just know I'm not staying until 5 in the morning, I'm too old for this." I add as we walked to the back of the gym.

"Well, my category is last to walk, so I gotta stay late," says Eman.

"I really don't think anybody was talking to you Eman, real talk," I say.

"Ok, what the hell is your problem nigga?"

"Please don't act like you don't know I'm pissed because you are fucking my little dude behind my back! I should not have picked you up! I should have made your ass walk!"

"If you had a problem with me, then I could have found another way to get here! You drove all the way here, and then you wait until we get inside to act dumb! I don't want that boy, you can have him! Your ass went behind my back in the first place. I introduced you to him, and you just wanna be a thirsty dick sucker."

"Bitch! How in the hell can you call me thirsty when you have sex with anything with a pulse? I know you probably got HIV."

"Nigga, I don't have no HIV! I always wrap it up, and I can show my papers with your jealous fat ass!"

"Will y'all stop now, please? I'm trying to feel my pill and my drink, and y'all bringing down my high," interjects Jay Jay.

"Truth be told, that boy fucking half of Detroit, and y'all sitting here arguing over him," adds Trayvon.

"I'm not arguing with Robert, he is a messy queen," says Eman.

"And you a messy hoe," I add.

How in the world can he call me messy when I have always been there for Eman? I pick his ass up all the time, and give him money when he needs it. He claims that Trayvon is his best friend, hell, I introduced them. I might be a lot of things, but I know for a fact I'm a good friend towards Eman. He is just ignorant as hell!

This night is already not starting off well considering that out of the four of us, only Trayon and Emmanuel walk these stupid ass balls. I am not in a house, and really don't like going to balls. I just don't get it. Vogueing is fun, but they can keep all this other shit! Who wants to be spending money to walk for a trophy that you might not win, and stay up until seven in the morning? That's dumb as fuck.

Sometimes, I forget they are still in high school, but I'm too grown for it. I'd much rather go to a pageant, than a ball. Honesty, fuck the ball or the pageant! I could be with a cute little young boy tonight, but instead I'm here at this gay shit trying to keep my so-called friends happy. This diva, Eman has some damn nerves. Never again!

"Robert, let's go to the bar and get a drink. I'll buy you one," says Jay Jay.

"That's good 'cause why y'all doing that, me and Eman going to the bathroom so I can get ready. Plus, I need to sniff me a vapor inhaler so I can feel my ecstasy pill," Trayvon adds.

"I think I took a dud because I don't feel nothing. I'm going to have to take two," Jay Jay interjects.

"Girl, you're a hardcore druggie," laughs Trayvon.

"And you one to talk! Bye girl, we going to bar," says Jay Jay as he grabs my hand and we proceed to the bar across the room.

"Jay Jay, you know we brought our own liquor. Why are you taking me to the bar to buy a drink?" I asked.

"Because I was getting tired of the tension between you and Eman."

"Well, it wasn't my fault."

"Didn't say it was, but you definitely knew Eman knew the boy first, so why go and fall for him."

"First of all, I didn't fall for the boy, he just has good dick. I don't even like him like that."

"All I'm sayin is that you and Eman need to slow down with all the dicks in the booty thing. And I know you don't like condoms, so why you sitting here trying to read Eman about some damn HIV? Hell, y'all having sex with the same boy, so if he got it then you got it."

"I ain't got shit!" I yell.

"I guess! Let's go the table so I can take my second pill," asked Jay Jay.

As the night went on, the crowd grew larger, and fine ass boys were everywhere. I only like coming to balls so I can see the sex siren and body categories. I'll make sure to have my camera phone ready when they hit the runway so I can take pictures. The legendary commentator is now on the microphone, and he starts to chant and call out several ballroom houses.

He calls out the House of Chanel, and a bunch of girls storm the runway. Then, he calls out the House of Mizrahi, and The Cash Money Boys. To me, these houses are nothing but gay black fraternities, or maybe even a gang that uses vogue and runway as the competition. I was told the names of these houses mainly came from actual names of fashion houses, while other people name their houses from original names and common interest. I'm literally standing here, scoping out the gym at all the fine ass men, when I hear two gunshots go off.

I immediately fell to the ground, not sure what the fuck was going on. I heard loud noises from people rushing to the doors, trying to get out, but my big ass stayed on the ground. I was always told when you hear gun shots, you get down, you don't run. The last thing you need is a bullet going through your back.

After a few minutes of not hearing another gunshot, I lifted my head, and I spotted Jay Jay just a few feet away from me under a table. I motion for him to crawl over to me, so we could plan how get the hell out. I tried to look around without completely getting up, and I can't see Eman, nor Trayvon. I knew they went to the bathroom to change clothes, but that's exactly where the gun shots sounded like they came from. I hope nothing happened to them. I know me and Eman are at each other's throat, but I don't want anything to happen to them. I am so fucking high, and my heart is beating out of control. I am wheezing hysterically and starting to sweat. Damn, I got to lose some weight!

Trayvon

Damn, I had barely started to get dressed for my category when I heard gunshots go off. Eman was yelling to hurry up and put my shoes on while he was yanking me out of the bathroom, and back into the gym. We rushed down the hallway to get out of the emergency exit. Everybody was running hysterically as we are tried to navigate outside of harm's way. At that point, I was terrified, but feeling a bit lucky that Eman was by my side and helping me get to the car.

It was hard to get through the mob of girls screaming and yelling, and as we walked through the door to go outside, even more gunshots went off. Then, I saw this infamous runway girl fall to the floor. There we were running out of the ball to get to safety, and we ran right into more bullets. Somebody shot this boy, and I'm thinking about what he could have done to get shot down in the middle of the street.

I instantly dropped to the ground and crawled behind a car, and that moment I noticed Eman was gone. We must have gotten separated during those second rounds of gunshots. I was sitting on the ground wondering what to do next. I just wasn't trying to get shot over something I had nothing to do with.

I felt the tears pouring down my face, thinking about the image of the boy's lifeless body lying on the ground. I didn't really know the boy, but we walked against each other at many balls. He was a cute little something. I wasn't attracted to him personally, but he had the bubbliest personality. He was very competitive when it came to walking balls, but being shot is just crazy. Ge Ge would be so mad at me right now. She is always so worried when I'm hanging out late with friends and look at me, two feet away from death.

We should be able to be safe around our own people. It's not enough we have to watch our backs from being bullied and beat on in school, but to think that even our gay brothers and sisters are a threat, is heartbreaking. God bless this boy's soul. I hope he doesn't die.

"Trayvon," yells Eman through the loud ass ambulance truck sirens.

"I'm over here behind the car," I respond back looking over the car to see Eman face.

"Lets go, I got us a ride to the crib."

"What about Jay Jay and Robert?"

"I told them to go ahead. You know damn well I wasn't getting back in the car after all that shit Robert was talking. Let's go to my crib".

"Are you sure? Are they okay? I need to see they're ok."

"They are ok. Come on before we get left. You coming to my house."

"Okay!"

I have known Eman for almost two years, and I have never been over his house before. I found it quite strange that he decided to come back here after all that drama that went down. I'm kinda mad about the thirty dollars I lost at the ball, but on the other hand, I'm relieved nothing happened to me. I just keep thinking about watching that boy fall to the ground and GeGe. She is going to kill me herself once she finds out what happened.

I bet she's going to see it on the news. She is so protective of me. I'm really glad Eman was there. It's so weird because all four of us were at that ball, but Eman was the only one they're for me when I needed him. He was always there for me.

Oh shit! I'm starting to get horny. I just remember after taking an ecstasy pill, I always get horny. I'm nervous because Eman chose such an intimate space to end the night. It's just me and him in a room, and alone in the middle of the night. I wasn't prepared for this.

"Boy, why are you still standing up? Take a sit on the bed," Eman aggressively asks entering back into his bedroom.

"Whatever, Emmanuel! It's not like I have ever been over here before. You were supposed to invite me to sit on your bed. Why you ain't got no chairs in here, anyway?"

"I don't know, maybe 'cause I'm just hood. Everything goes down in my bed."

"I bet! Actually, I know. I've heard stories about this room. Look at the infamous dark black curtains."

"It ain't even like that. I just like my room dark when I smoke my weed. You wanna hit this blunt?"

"You know I don't smoke weed, but this pill is making me wanna smoke tonight. I'm gonna be high as fuck!"

"Yay!"

"Yay, nothing. Are you mad you didn't get a chance to walk the ball tonight?"

"Nah, not really. I got so much on my mind right now, I really could care less about a ball right now."

"Like what?"

"Hell, I graduate next week, and I don't know what I want to do with my life. Plus, I'm broke, and I'm not working."

"You will figure it out, and get the money somehow."

"Not necessarily, Trayvon. My mom can't take care of me like how your grandma takes care of you. I got to hustle to survive, and plus I got to figure out how to take care of moms now"

"What you mean? Why would you have to take care of her?"

"She got cancer."

"What? Eman, I am so sorry to hear that. How long have you known?"

"About a year, man. Just being real low-key about it. I didn't want to get everybody involved."

"But it's me, you could have told me so I could have been there for you."

"Boy, you too young to be here for me. You don't have time to help me. You need to focus on school, and make sure you graduate. I mean, I do apologize for not telling you, though."

"Do Jay Jay or Robert know?"

"I told Jay Jay. You know he so easy to talk to."

"Yeah, he is."

"Anyway, let's change the subject; this is bringing my high down."

"Is that the Aaliyah song, 'At Your Best' playing from your computer?"

"Yeah, I downloaded it the other day on LimeWire. I love this song!"

"*At Your Best*" by our hometown princess, Aaliyah, is hands down my favorite song of all time! I'm not sure if Eman knew that or not, but this is just a perfect song to vibe to with the perfect person. This song is so beautiful, and it makes me dream about being in love. I know I'm pretty young, but I have a thing about being married with kids, and a perfect home. I fantasize for hours about having the perfect guy and being so happy. I am just a relationship-type of dude.

"What you know about love?" I blurted out, snapping out of my daydream.

"Not too much. I have only loved two dudes so far. The first guy I've ever had sex with, and you."

"Aww! I love you too, Eman. You know everybody swear I got a big crush on you."

"You do, and that's okay because I got a crush on you, too. If I wasn't such a little hoe, I would have tried to boo you up."

"You not a hoe, you just a freak!"

"Boy, shut up! Let's cuddle together, and I'm gonna sneak and play with your booty."

"You won't be doing all that, but cuddling sounds cool."

"Get over here then, you my bff with benefits tonight," says Eman as he pulls me closer to him on top of his bed.

"What makes you happy?"

"That's a loaded question. I really don't know. I am happy right now with you."

"I am happy, too. You make me feel loved."

"I try to, Tray. I know it's hard for us to get love from anybody out here. You are a sweetheart. You deserved to be loved."

"When I think about it, I've never had love from a man before. I don't know my daddy, My stepfather hated me, and I don't have any brothers. Luckily, we got each other to love on since the world can't give it to us."

"It's like a blessing that God has given us to protect our heart."

"Your body feels so good holding me like this. Are you falling asleep?"

"Yeah, I'm dozing off a bit. I need to because if I don't, I'm going to fuck you, Trayvon. I want you bad."

"It's not time, yet."

"I know."

"Love you."

"Love you too Tray."

Eman

One of my favorite places in the world to hang out is on Jay Jay's back porch at night. It's a nice little covered porch, decorated with four chairs, two patio tables, and two mood setting lanterns. He would usually invite one of us over for a drink, and before we knew it, all four of us were sitting on the porch talking shit to one another. Even if one us were having an issue with another one, we usually didn't address it, and just let it boil up until it exploded on a night when we were all drunk.

Liquor tends to always give us a license to share our feelings, which always lead to major drama. During the last couple of years of school, I was invited to a lot of after school events, or dance parties at the school, but I would always decline. Female and male classmates were always trying to take me out, but I just didn't want to go. Even though I'm a student, I really don't hang out with high schools kids besides Trayvon.

I don't know if it's because we don't have much in common, or maybe it's just because I just rather be with grown folks. Either way, I usually found a reason to make my way over to Jay Jay's house everyday by 6 p.m. Most times, we didn't do anything but watch television. It's like my home away from home. It didn't help that we both live off 7 mile, and he is just a bus ride away.

His momma is always telling us we're too loud, and he always yelling back being crazy. Yep! This is my hang out spot. Today, we just ended up over here because we all are planning a trip to D.C. for a ball, and we had to figure who was driving, and who will have their damn money. The last trip we took together was a disaster. We went to Cincinnati, and let's just say things didn't go according to our plan.

Robert got into a car accident on the way down there, and basically was a bitch the whole weekend because he knew his momma was going to chew him out about it. We argued the whole trip, and I almost blacked his eye. Jay Jay came down without any money, and didn't have enough for his part for hotel room. He seems to always cry broke, but he somehow finds money to do the things he want to do for himself.

Trayvon missed his category because we were late getting to the ball. He spent weeks working on his effect for the category, and he never got a chance to wear it. He had a cute little attitude all weekend, too. It was a horrible trip, and we felt it was best to start planning our trip so it wouldn't happen again.

"I'm letting you hoes know now, I'm not driving the whole way," says Robert

"Bitch! Nobody else want to drive your momma's car so you can be acting all scary and being a back seat driver," Jay Jay adds.

"Well, who told your ass to drive a hundred miles an hour in a seventy five after I already crashed her car? That's just reckless Ms. Thing."

"You know I drive fast when I take a pill. I get a lead foot."

"How you about you make sure you pay us all our money before we leave so we don't have any troubles?," I ask as I try to pass Jay Jay the blunt I just rolled up.

"Get that away from me! You know I don't smoke weed. I only do old white lady drugs. I am cunt," interjects Jay Jay

"Girl, your shape looks like an old white lady!"

"Bitch please! You wish, and I don't think I'm going to D.C."

"Why not?" Asks Trayvon.

"Y'all not about to be reading me over my coins. I might not have enough."

"Jay Jay, girl I know you got at least one hundred dollars in the musty bra you got on," Robert laughs.

"Don't play honey, this bra and pantie set is from Victoria's Secret. Your man bought it for me."

"I guess we'll go without. Anyway, did y'all hear about those girls getting evicted out that house up the street?" I asked, trying to change the subject.

"Girl, I heard it was five people living in that little one bedroom house," says Robert.

"Yeah, it is a tiny house, but I heard his best friend was sleeping with his boyfriend. I think it's his fault because I be damned if I have my man living with three other girls in a one bedroom," says Jay Jay.

"Girl, from what I heard, they were in an open relationship. They always having threesomes and orgies in that house," Trayvon adds.

"Yeah that's true. I had a threesome with them last year, and their roommates kept coming in and out the bedroom while we was fucking, so I told them to just join," I confessed.

"Bitch, you so nasty! I knew I saw you running out that house. So, is the boy dick uncircumcised? Everybody talking about the boy walking around with a turtle neck on," Robert asks.

"Oh my God, here we go again! Yes, his dick was uncircumcised, and so is mines. What the hell is the big deal? The real issue was that the house they were living in had no furniture, or a bed. It was five of us on an air mattress on the floor."

"Chile, they just trifling. Why have people over to your place and you don't have anywhere for a bitch to sit? I mean, I don't have anything against an uncircumcised penis., I just never had one before,"Trayvon says.

"Girl, I guess some people are clean, but I heard it be all kinds of smells and nastiness underneath all that extra skin. I had one guy who was uncircumcised, but we just had sex. I wasn't putting all that in my mouth," chimes in Jay Jay.

"I wish a bitch would deny giving me head. My dick stays clean," I added just let these hoes know.

"Ok girl, wasn't anybody talking about you. But did y'all here about how they went to jail for domestic abuse?"

"Yeah, I did. Nowadays, they can put both of the people in a same sex relationship in jail. The police don't be playing with these girls. I just don't understand how you can be in a relationship, and fighting each other. I'll just have to break up," says Trayvon.

"I don't, either. You put your hands on me, and you are my lover, I'm going to shoot your ass!" I add.

"I don't know about that, I like all that rough play. Throw me up against the wall, and then tear my walls up," says Jay Jay.

"I agree with Jay Jay. Ain't nothing like having a fight, and then having makeup sex right after. That shit is hot," Robert says while heading the bottle of liquor to make another dink.

"I guess it's an older girl thing because I don't want any parts of that. Can you make a drink without putting a bunch of orange juice in it?" Trayvon asks.

"Bitch, do I look like Florida Evans? Why you making requests and shit? I don't put a lot of juice in your cup, your ass is just a lush!" Robert says.

"Actually, you do look like Florida Evans, so be quiet."

"Bitch, who watched last night's episode of Sex and the City?" Jay Jay asks

"Girl, I did. It was so good. That argument between Miranda and Carrie was epic."

"Yes, it was! Miranda is always so negative about other people's decisions."

"That's true, but Miranda is the realest, and she just be stating facts. Carrie don't have no business running off to Paris to be with that old man."

"I know right! I don't want her with him, either. She needs to get back with Mr. Biggs. I just know they're going to end up together again."

"Y'all always getting caught up in those girlie shows. Y'all already got me watching Charmed. Hell will freeze over before my ass sit down and watch some damn Sex and the City," I interrupt.

"I don't see why not. You are clearly the main one around here having sex all over the city. You should relate," Jay Jay laughs.

"Bitch, how you relate to your mama needing to repave this driveway? Looking like y'all live in the projects!"

"Girl, I rather it look like we are in the projects, than to actually be born and raised in the projects like your ass! Let me borrow your bridge card."

"Whatever, bitch!"

It's never a dull moment with these hating hoes.

Robert

I had to stop fucking around with that young dude me and Eman fell out over. That nigga was dumb as hell. I was buying all his shoes, and keeping money in his pocket, and he still wanted to mess around with Eman's broke ass. These young dudes play too many stupid games. I just get caught up with their big dicks.

For some reason, all the young skinny boys be having the biggest dick, and that's my krypronite. I get weak. I recently met this fine ass dude who rides my shuttle from the bus stop to his job at the food court in the airport. We've been having small talk everyday on my shuttle about random shit, and I could never tell if he was straight or gay. I knew he had a big dick though because one day he wore some grey sweatpants, and I could see his dick hanging down his leg and I had to have it.

A couple of weeks ago, I got bold and asked him if he wanted a car. I knew the nigga was tired of catching the bus back and forth to work everyday. He told me he would do anything for a car. So, I told his ass all he had to do was fuck me raw, and I would co-sign for a car and pay the note every month. Of course, he said he was down.

He started catching his bus up here at the end of my route, so he could be the last passenger to get on the shuttle, and we been fucking on the shuttle the last few weeks. I usually found a spot in the airport parking lot, turned off all of the lights in the shuttle, and started sucking his dick. The first time he pulled out all eleven inches, I sucked him until I felt all of his babies in the back of my throat. The nigga can bust like four to five nuts in one session, and I catch them all.

The last time he came up here, he had me pinned down on the back row of the shuttle with my knees in the seats, and my hand up on the wall. He was pounding me as he was gripping the bars of the luggage compartment up top. He shot his last nut at least twenty feet across the shuttle and all I could think about was who was cleaning it up because I wasn't. Damn, he got the best dick I ever had.

Yesterday, after picking up his car, I asked the nigga if he wanted to go on a date to celebrate his new car, and the mother-fucker told me no. I asked him why not, and he said he doesn't date big dudes. At first, I got mad because I get tired of niggas dissing me because I am fat, but then I asked the nigga why he was fucking my fat ass then, and he said because he needed a car.

"Bitch, I'm burning!" I said as I came out of the bathroom in my momma basement talking to Jay Jay.

"Girl, what the hell are you talking about?"

"Bitch, it burns when I pee, and my dick hurts so bad. What you think that I mean?"

"Honey, I came over here to burn a CD on your computer, not to be your medical provider. Do I look like Doogie Howser, M.D.?"

"Bitch! Stop playing, I'm in pain."

"Well, who you think burned you anyway?"

"I don't know. I just started messing around with this dude on my shuttle, and I have been trolling Palmer Park at night, fuck-ing in the woods."

"Ugh, girl you are nasty. You been fucking everybody! I hear stories about what goes down in those woods. How you gone know who burned you, miss hot pants?"

"I know, right. I can't figure who to stop fucking."

"Robert, how about you stop fucking everybody until you figure out what is going on? And when did your ass start using your dick? I thought you was a bottom, like me?"

"I met this little high school boy who has a fetish for big boys, so I've been sucking him off, and then topping him. I don't like it, though. My dick never stays hard."

"You still messing around with boys in high school? You gone go to jail."

"If they old enough to pee, then they old enough for me."

"You are a pervert, and you need to take your ass to the clinic instead of indulging me in your illegal sexcapades."

"Girl, I'm scared!"

"Scared of what?"

"That I got something!"

"Duh, bitch! You probably do, Mr. King Raw of Detroit, but you still need to go find out! Knowing your status is better than not knowing."

"Bitch, miss me with that safe sex campaign bullshit!"

"Fine. Don't go to the doctor, and let your dick fall off. You don't need it anyway. I'm getting mines removed, too. I'm a lady."

"Shut up, bitch! You so stupid! I've been taking these over the counter UZI tablets that have been making my piss turn orange. At first, they were working, now they don't. It says I'm only supposed to take them for two days, but I've been taking them for over two weeks."

"That's stupid! Take your ass to the the doctor for real, and help me burn this damn CD. Your limewire never works. You probably got too much porn on this computer."

"Chile, what CD you trying to burn anyways?"

"Ashanti."

"Ashanti? Ja Rule's Ashanti? Bitch, her voice is horrible, and she got thick ass sideburns!"

"Girl I like it. The album is cunt to me. I want her album, and Tweet's new album."

"How about you go buy them, then?"

"Girl, you know I don't buy CD's. I'm cheap. Why buy it if I can download it on your computer for free?"

"You late!"

"Whatever, bitch! Now, your burning red hot sausage link is what's late," says Jay Jay as he laughs his ass off.

Jay Jay

What the fuck? Why is that I can't never find a man? I am so tired of meeting all these lame dudes on Black Planet and BG-Clive. It always starts off good when we're talking online, but when it's actually time to meet up in person, that's when the shit hits the fan. It's already hard to find a dude that like feminine boys, but nowadays the ones that do like feminine boys think that I'm desperate.

They think they are doing me a favor because they don't have "No Fem , No Fats" posted on their pages. Bitch please! Most of those dudes don't have a car, or they live at home with their momma. We can't have a serious relationship if we both live at home with our mommas. I am not fucking in your momma car, and you not coming over here to fuck in my momma's basement. Really, we ain't fucking... period!

Why can't I find a guy that wants to take me out to dinner, or to the movies without wanting some ass in return? Is that too much to ask? I think the last time I went on a real date was with my last boyfriend, Deangelo, about two years ago. I thought he was the one until I found out he was the biggest whore in Detroit.

Eman, Travyon, and Robert all told me he was making flirty passes at them while we were together. I didn't deserve that shit, so I politely broke up with him and told him to lose my number. I just want to be loved without being cheated on. I've always imagined that I would get married to this fine ass masculine dude, and we would live in a house with a white picket fence in the suburbs. We would adopt two Asian babies, have great sex, and live happily ever after. The older I get, the less that seems like reality. Instead I have to get past all of the dudes who don't like Fem boys, and get past all of the scrubs who only want me for my body.

Now, when I agreed to have this damn graduation party at my house, I would have never thought I'd be cooking the whole menu myself. I have already cooked my infamous five layered macaroni and cheese, greens, and fried chicken. Now, Eman wants me to cook a pineapple upside down cake. Everybody knows I'm the best cook, but Trayvon could have at least helped with the barbecue! Lazy Ass!

Hell, he wasn't the only one at the club all night. Luckily, I'm still high from the ecstasy pill I took last night, and decided to take a few bumps of coke this morning to stay up. Of course, my momma got an attitude because she says it's too many niggas running in and out of her kitchen. She really just wish that the attention was all on her, and that she was in this kitchen cooking. She wants all of my friends to say she can cook. I keep telling her all of my friends have already tasted her cooking, so she needs to just find some business, and some friends, too.

I just can't wait until I move to Atlanta, so I can live my life. I've been working on my vision board about all the things I want to accomplish once I move. I want to get back into fashion school, and work for a fashion blog. I want to start really dating guys that are into me. I'm done with going back and forth with all these boys who don't know what they want. I need a man. I need a real man.

"Girl, do you need me to go to the store, and get another bottle of Bacardi?" asks Robert as he walked into the kitchen.

"Naw, Trayvon and I went to the store earlier and bought three bottles. You gotta go get them out my momma's car," I added.

"Oh, okay, I need to make me another drink, and ain't nothing but dark liquor downstairs, and I ain't trying to get sick."

"What is Trayvon doing anyway? Why he ain't helping me in this kitchen? He swears Eman is his best friend, so his ass should be helping. I didn't say I was going to do everything."

"Really, girl? You already knew his hot-in-the-pants ass was not going to help you in this kitchen. He is downstairs playing spades anyway."

"Why you ain't playing with them?"

"You know I'm trying to keep my distance from Eman. It's his day, and I am not trying to cause any drama. I'm just being cordial in your momma's house, and sipping on my drinks."

"Oh my God! Are you still on that, Robert? Are you and that boy still even messing around?"

"No, we're not. We broke up, but that's not the point. I am really just tired of being disrespected as a friend. Hell, I introduced him to Trayvon, and it seems like they just pushed me to the side."

"Are you serious, Robert? I thought we graduated from high school six years ago. So why are you acting like a young queen? We are all friends. I'm just as close with you as I am with them. They just have more in common because they are closer in age, and they like each other. You really just mad that Trayvon is in love with Eman, and not you."

"Please! Why in the hell would I care about who that boy is in love with?"

"I don't know, Robert, you tell me because I don't get it. I know you liked him when you first brought him around, but we have all gotten so close as friends, why would you care?"

"I don't care. My issue is with Eman and how he treats our friendship. I've been over Trayvon years ago."

"I guess. Will you go and get the liquor out of my momma's car, and let me finish in this kitchen?"

"Yeah. It's too damn hot in here, anyway," says Robert as he exits the house by the side door.

I swear I just don't understand Robert sometimes. We have been friends since high school, and he is still going through the same thing; jealously. I'm talking about that deep down in the soul type jealously. We have never really had that issue because he has never been attracted to me. I've always been too cunt for him. He likes boys who can pass as straight, and I am the furthest from that.

When we were in high school, he would always fall in love with guys that were too old for him. And now that we're older, he keeps trying to fall in love with guys that are much younger than him. He's really insecure about his weight. He has been trying to lose weight for over six years, and he has steadily gotten bigger. I believe because of me being such a queen, and him being kinda fat, is how we actually got so close.

We both had to fight people all through school to defend ourselves against bullies, and trust me, we used to whoop ass in the process! Okay, I'm lying. We got our ass whooped all the time. I don't know how to fight, and I was scared that someone was going to pull all my hair out, and I would have just died if that happened.

Robert is such a great friend, but he never seems to be happy. He is always looking for love from these dudes, and Trayvon was another one he loved at first sight. He brought him around saying he was his new young little piece. I knew something was strange about it, and of course, Trayvon was not attracted to him. So, they became girlfriends and never had any sexual encounters.

Eventually, we all began to hang out and stuff, and it seems like overnight, all four of us became really close. We actually call ourselves the Ya-Ya Sisterhood (after the movie). Even though I end up being the mediator between all of their shit. I love my girls.

" Y'all bitches ready?" I yell as I go to the CD player to play Destiny's Child Writing on the Wall album.

"Get in place ladies. Remember, I'm Beyoncé, and we can divide lines up between the four of us."

All of us get up in our "Bills, Bills, Bills" pose, and proceed to sing the lyrics to the song in front of everyone in my momma's basement. It was time to put on a fucking show.

"At first we started off as cool," I start off

"Taking me places I ain't never been," says Robert.

"But now you getting comfortable, ain't doing those things you did no more," adds Trayvon

"You're slowly making me pay for things, your money should be handling," Eman adds.

We continue to sings song from that entire album, even doing some of our favorite tracks off of their "Survivor" album. Even though I am tired as fuck from all that damn cooking, this is the best time we had in a minute. I love house parties in general, I just hate when I have to be up all morning cleaning shit because my momma would kill me if I tried to sleep in with her house being a mess.

Everyone seems to be enjoying the vibe and inviting more and more people over to this house. I've been outside giving directions all night, and before I know it, half of the party is happening up and down my block. I know my neighbors are having a field day watching all these queens drive up and down the street. Hell, they should be used to the gays considering I like to cut the grass in my momma's daisy dukes every other week. And I see how the boys be staring, driving by and about to get in car accident. They be wanting all this body.

"You can't block my neighbor's driveway motherfuckers!" This is definitely about to be a great night.

Eman

I cannot get my graduation party out of my head. It's been over three weeks, but I have to say, it was the party of all parties! We literally shut Jay Jay's block down. His neighbors called the police on us twice, and we eventually had to tell people to start going home.

Some people got caught sucking dick in the bathroom, and doing coke. I even got head outside by some cute boy while smoking my blunt. I had gone to the side of the house to clear my head and smoke my blunt, and this guy I've known for some time came up to me asking if I wanted some birthday head.

At first, I said no because I knew Tray was in the house and I didn't want him to catch me. But this boy was dark and sexy as fuck, and I love dark-skinned boys. Probably one of the reasons I be all up in Tray's face. This boy was short as fuck with the phattest ass, dimples, and three sixty waves in his hair. The nigga was even bow-legged.

We took a few hits on my blunt, and then, I let him slob me up. The nigga was sucking me off like his life depended on. Of course, I returned the favor with my tongue in his booty cheeks, and maybe a poke or two. I was still worried about anybody seeing me, so I didn't go all the way.

Afterwards, we kept the party going with a game of spoons and shady hearts. Robert even pulled me to the side to work on our issues. I was so fucked up, I believe we decided to let go of our beef, and decided to count it as water under the bridge. I still will keep my guard up, but now I know what Robert is capable of when he's angry.

I just always hoped he didn't do anything really crazy to me like I have seen him do to others. I hope our friendship stops him from crossing the line, and so far, so good. I just feel like he is the harder on me than he is with Trayvon and Jay Jay. He is always coming for me, and talking shit. When I talk shit back, he can't take it.

He's always trying to compete with me when dealing with boys and I have to remind him, I'm a stripper and escort. I know everybody in Detroit's gay scene on a sexual tip, and there is no competition. He is usually always complaining about his weight, and I would tell him, bitch do something about it! Actually, he must have done something lately because his big ass is losing weight.

I really hate hospitals! I hate the smell of latex. I hate how cold it usually is. I hate how loud it is during the day with patients and staff moving around like chickens with their heads cut off. I really hate the night time when it's dead quiet, and you can hear feet squeak against the shining floors as the machine beeps every second.

I hate that mom has to be here! I hate she was diagnosed with cancer last year and things are now turning for the worst. I hate the idea of my mom not being able to come home this time. I'm just so full hate, but I have to stay hopeful and pray for my mom's healing.

"Emmanuel can you go downstairs to the vending machine and get me a Snickers bar? I want something sweet," ask mom from the hospital bed.

"Okay ma. Let's wait until the nurse comes back in, and we can ask her if it's okay," I tell her.

"Listen here, boy! I don't need the nurse's permission to tell me if I can have a Snickers or not. I have been in and out the hospital all year. I think I know what I can eat."

"I know ma, but now you can't stop throwing up blood. You had blood coming out your nose and mouth at the same time. That ain't never happened before."

"What did I say?"

"Ma, you acting like nothing is going on right now."

"It's something going on, but I'm still hungry."

"Ma!"

"Okay I'm sorry. I mean, Emmanuel, I am really scared. Hell, I didn't think I did all this chemotherapy to just end up bleeding to death."

"Ma, please don't talk like that. I really can't take you talking like that."

"I know baby, I am trying to stay strong for you."

"Don't stay strong for me, stay strong for yourself."

"I don't have much more fight for myself anymore. All I have is the fight to stay strong for you."

"Well, stay strong lady. It ain't time to give up! I need you here, ma! You all I got."

"I'm still here, Emmanuel, and I am still waiting on my Snickers. Now, go downstairs and get my damn candy bar!"

"Okay, ma, I'm going."

The thought of losing my mom is so devastating to me. I am the only child, and I have a weird relationship with my family. I haven't seen my birth father since I was five. He went off and got the lady down the street pregnant, and then he moved to another neighborhood with his new family. Word on the street is that he's a crack head, now.

I thought I saw him coming out of one of those infamous crack houses one day, but I wasn't sure. I was riding my bike through the alley, and yelled his name once I approached the corner house, but the man just kept walking. The only memories I actually have of him is because of pictures we took when I was a kid. I remember going to visit his side of the family for a few years after he left, but I ended that once I got older. It didn't make sense to keep a relationship with the family of a man that wasn't around to be my father.

I was closer to my mom's side of the family. I grew up with all my cousins and aunt, but most members of my family don't accept me being gay, and they have completely distanced themselves from me. All of the cousins I grew up with, played basketball with, and helped sneak girls in the house for, didn't even wish me well on my graduation. So, if she leaves this earth, it literally would be me trying to survive in this world by myself. I haven't told too many people about her illness, mainly just Trayvon and Jay Jay, and they have been supportive, so I guess that's enough love for little ole me.

Trayvon

There was another female body found in the alley today on the eastside. This time, it was actually one of my classmates, and the whole school was sad. The girl had been missing for a week, so most of us expected foul play, but the fact she was found naked, raped, and dead, sends fear throughout the school.

There are random girls walking around the hallways crying, and I would see them just fall to the ground and start wailing in the hallway. This shit makes my heartache. There has been a string of black, teenage girls going missing, and she is just one of the latest found dead. These girls are disappearing while in route to school, or on their way home from school as they pass through downtown.

It's just not safe in this city anymore, and that's why I try to keep my ass away from downtown when it's dark. I ride the bus to school and back home almost every single day, and I have seen all types of crazy shit. A few months ago, a man threatened me and my home girl because we told the police that we saw him pick-pocketing folks at our bus stop. We saw him doing it for weeks and didn't say anything, but once I saw him pickpocket that old lady, I had to say something,

He came up to us after seeing us talking to the police at the bus stop on Woodward, and yelled out that he was going to fuck us up. We ended up finding another police officer on Warren Ave, and told him what the dude said. He suggested that we switch up our bus route if we could for the sake of our own protection.

I started carrying a knife to school with me, and would hide it in the bushes in the mornings so I could walk through the metal detectors without any problems. I wasn't gangsta enough to carry a gun, but I needed something for protection and I wasn't taking any chances. Being a gay black boy, or any type of girl, walking through these streets easily puts a target on our backs. Every day, our lives are in danger, whether we think so or not.

I kept hearing my mother and GeGe talk about the good ole days here in the city. The days where everybody knew each other in the neighborhood, and everybody was like family. All the kids could play late outside at night without any issues, and how everybody left their doors unlocked. This definitely hasn't been my reality since I've been born, and I couldn't imagine it being that safe.

GeGe always said the crack epidemic, and the riots in the neighborhoods changed the city, and it never recovered. She might be right because catching the bus through the city, I've been able to see all of the abandoned buildings, and drug addicts hanging out on the corners. I fantasize about the good ole days they speak of, and wonder what the hell happened. Growing up here looks no different than the ruined cities in the Middle East during war. Total devastation!

I told this older guy that I work with at White Castle about what was happening at the bus stop, and he volunteered to walk me to GeGe's apartment every night we worked together. He was an older dude, and I usually don't like older dudes, but I really like his humor and flirty ways.

His name was Carlos. He was thick built, but solid, and wasn't bad on the eyes. He was really a funny guy. A guy who can make me laugh always had a chance to get, and keep my attention. Nobody at work knew he was gay, and they especially didn't know that he was messing around with a minor. I kept what was going on with us to myself because I didn't want to get him in trouble. I didn't mention it to Jay Jay or Robert, either, and definitely not Eman. He wouldn't have liked that shit at all.

"Why did you keep mopping my feet with that dirty ass mop water at work?" I asked as Carlos and I were walking home from work.

"Hey, first of all, that water wasn't dirty. I made that water myself with bleach. Hell, I was trying to get your attention. You've been ignoring me all day," Carlos responds.

"You used that same nasty mop that we have been using since I started there. It's nasty."

"What's wrong with you little dude?"

"I don't know. Keep thinking about my classmate and shit. Her funeral was today, and I didn't go. I was too scared."

"Why were you scared?"

"Honestly, I don't know. I think I was scared to see her face. I don't like dead bodies."

"I feel that. I used to be like that."

"What changed?"

"I went to jail, little nigga. Being in there, and seeing the shit you see, makes you look at the world different."

"Yeah, I bet, but at least you had a roof over your head."

"What? Little nigga, you can't be that naïve to think jail is a good place to be. I gave up five years of my life to the white man."

"Nah, that's not what I am saying. I'm just saying that it is some people who don't have a home, or somewhere to sleep. I see a lot of homeless, gay boys when I go up to the Ruth Ellis Center. Technically, before I lived with G-Ge, I was homeless.

"Hell, I would rather live on the street, than to be in prison. I used to think like you do, though."

"What made you change?"

"People started dying, and I wasn't able to go to the funerals, and pay my respects. Man, I've lost so many homies on the block from selling drugs and shit. My cousin, who I grew up with, got popped last year and I couldn't go to his funeral. That shit hurts!"

"Damn, that is fucked up! Man, I forgot you been to prison before, and you be in these streets hanging with all the straight boys."

"It's not even about that, though. I got gay homies that's gone, too. You got to remember, I'm about fifteen years older than you, and I've had so many homies pass away from gay shit while I was in prison. People die. You'll see. Just watch and wait."

"I don't want to see. I don't want any of my friends to die."

"It's life, little dude. We all gotta die."

"Yeah we do, but we ain't gotta get murdered and raped, or die from AIDS."

"You right! Life's a bitch, sometimes. I spent five years hating life, but don't focus on that. Life is good, too. It ain't all that bad."

"Yeah, it ain't all bad. I got good friends. I got you."

"Word! You got me, huh? You flirting with me little dude?"

"No, I am not. I like somebody else."

"I don't care if you like another dude. You like me, too. I can tell."

"I might."

"You do," he says as he grabs my face, and sticks his tongue down my throat.

"Nigga, I didn't say you could do that. I told you about being all rough and stuff."

"You didn't tell me I couldn't, either, with your sexy little ass."

"Well, I'm telling you now. I don't like it."

"Okay. I'm sorry little nigga, dang. You inviting me in, or what?" he asks as we approached GeGe's patio door.

"I don't know, it's late, and I got school in the morning."

"Come on, little dude. I got a few hours until I have to catch the last bus home. You remember how much you liked it last time I came in?"

"Yeah, it felt good, but I ain't trying to get in trouble. You ain't supposed to be here."

"I'll come through the window like last time. Let me suck that big dick of yours."

"I don't know."

"Please!"

"Ok nigga, let me go inside, and I'll unlock my bedroom window. And be quiet, nigga. You can't wake my grandma up!"

I'm so glad its Friday. I had been craving a drink all week, and when Jay Jay called me to go the club Inuendo, I got dressed in ten minutes. I was bored siting in the house, and I was tired of thinking about death and shit. I just needed a cocktail and a dance floor to clear my mind.

I love dancing to release energy, and to move my body. I am not the one to stand in the corner and watch others have fun, and I can't stand no wallflower. I like to be the life of the party, and get everyone else to have a good time as well. Lately, I have been dancing like a stripper when I came to this club, and I can't figure out why.

I like to pop my booty and get on the ground, and put on a performance. I really don't care who sees me, and I don't care if people get mad because they thought I was more masculine. I am gay, so I feel like it doesn't matter if I'm masculine, feminine, top or bottom. I like boys, and I like the boys that I like. I don't get caught up in those roles you should play, depending on what you do in the bedroom sexually. I like ass but that doesn't mean I can't shake my ass, and it doesn't mean I am not a man. Jay Jay and I definitely have different opinions regarding this topic.

"If you climbing my back, you ain't gone be walking around in no pants tighter than mines," says Jay Jay as we are waiting at the bar to get another drink.

"Bitch! His pants don't make him no more masculine when the lights are off. He can wear baggy pants, and still be a lady. I mean look at you in these jogging pants. You ain't a masculine, and bitch, you never went to Michigan State, so I don't know why you wearing that hoodie."

"I fucked a boy that went to Michigan State, and he gave me a souvenir. You better belief he was 100% a top."

"Girl, there ain't no hundred percent tops," Eman adds, as he joins us at the bar.

"Speak for yourself. Everybody ain't down with all that flip-flop shit. I would never use my penis," says Jay Jay.

"Then cut it off then. The best sex is verse sex. Flip-flop all day long. It doesn't make sense to me to be gay, and don't like dick."

"I agree. I hate when boys even ask me if I am top or a bottom. I let them know that I am whatever they ain't. Verse sex is the best sex," I add.

"Whatever! I am a lady, and a bottom. I don't need no confusion in the bedroom. I don't want no nigga putting his ass up in the air waiting on me to do nothing with it. All I can do is show the nigga the door to get the hell out," laughs Jay Jay.

By the time midnight struck, my ass was drunk as a skunk. I had danced for two straight hours, and had two hours worth of cocktails. I was having a good time, and my ass kept trying to jump on the stage with the strippers. I never understood why clubs have the ugliest strippers. I mean, its cute boys all over this city with some great ass bodies, and they always managed to get boys with little to no bodies with bullet holes or war wounds all on their body.

My liquor was giving me enough courage to make me think I could do a better job. As the dancer was working the pole, I decided to jump on the stage and give him a helping hand. Before I began to drop it low, the security pulled me off the stage. I instantly got pissed, and waited for about five more minutes, and then I preceded to get on the stage again. Before I could even get my second leg on the stage, this big ass security guard rushes the stage and body slams me to the floor.

"Hey, man, I told you twice already that you can't be up there," yells the security guard.

"I heard what you said, nigga, but there wasn't no reason for you to put your hands on me, I know that fucking much," I respond pissed off.

"Okay, calm down, Tray. You are a little drunk, so take it easy. You know you can't get up there on stage while the strippers up there," says Eman as he looks in my eyes trying to read my mood.

"You better get your boy before he gets fucked up, talking all his shit," the security guard says.

"Come on man, he drunk. Now, we don't want any trouble, but you better back the fuck up out his face," says Eman as he got between the security guard and I.

"I'm going to walk away before I hit y'all in y'all smart ass mouths. Y'all gone get it," he says as he walks back to his post at the front door.

"Fuck him! I don't know why this stupid club keeps hiring straight men to be guards at a gay club. You know they don't like gay people. They just working here to get a check."

"Trayvon, are you okay. I wasn't trying to fight tonight. Ya drunk ass bout to get us jumped."

"I think I need some water."

"I can get you some water, and I'm going to find Jay Jay and Robert, so we can leave. I'm pissed about that security guard and I know they about to start some shit."

Eman, Jay Jay, and Robert came back with some water while I was sitting in the corner trying to sober up. I had to take a seat immediately because the room started spinning, and I felt like I had to throw up. I hadn't been this drunk in a very long time. As much as I was having a good time, I definitely was ready to home.

Eman decided it was best that we left, so he helped me up as we proceeded to leave out the club. As we reached the door, the dusty security guard pointed at another guy and began talking shit. And before I could gather my thoughts, I pushed the guy to the ground. Between my drunkenness, and his disrespect, I had taken enough of the bullshit.

I'm usually the mild-tempered one, but I think I really did feel like fighting, Again this is the liquor talking. The next thing I knew, Eman and I had been drugged out the club into the front lawn, and we were going head up with at least four security guards. I don't even know where all these damn security guards even came from.

Jay Jay and Robert were headed towards the car, trying to break it up, and trying to get us to leave with them. We all know those girls can't fight. I just remembered taking my coat off ,and trying to fight each dude one-on-one, but it wasn't working. We are outnumbered by these big ass dudes. Before I could figure out what direction to run to get back to the car, I was hit right in my face, and I fell to the ground.

"Trayvon," yells Robert

"Oh my God! He is not responding," yells Jay Jay

"Trayvon get up,"says Eman

"Trayvon!"

"Trayvon!"

"Trayvon!"

I literally remember gaining consciousness after hearing my name being yelled over and over again, and I woke up instantly with a horrible headache. I tried to stand up, but the ground started moving, and I instantly fell back down to the ground. It took me a minute to realize that these niggas literally knocked my drunken ass out. All three of the guys carried me to the car as Eman and I was dripping in blood with swollen faces. Damn, I'm never drinking again!

Robert

Well, it seems I won't need surgery after all. I have been losing weight for a while now, and I am not sure why. Of course I might have HIV, but I don't want to go to that conclusion, first. It could be something totally different, and a lot worse. I am not a person who likes to go the doctor, but my mom has been so worried about me. I've been burning for weeks, so I decided to make a trip to the local clinic out in the suburbs.

I definitely wasn't going downtown so I could run into somebody, and they start spreading rumors about my status. So, I decided to go out to Dearborn to check what was going on. HIV status is a like a weapon in these streets, and I didn't want to go where anyone could see me. I know they do free testing down at the Ruth Ellis Center, but I don't trust them. People act like getting HIV is a joke, but this shit been killing us for over thirty years! It's been killing us way before I came into this gay life.

I know the whole preventative concept of using a condom, and practicing safe sex, but I just don't like to use condoms. It doesn't feel good. When I'm getting dick, I like to feel the flesh and the warmth. It's not fair when straight people have unprotected sex, they can get babies, but when we do it, our lives are at risk. Our sexual behaviors are no different than what they're doing, but we're often looked at as being nasty and freaky.

Men are whores, straight or gay. When I started to have sex, I knew I was going to get HIV. Everybody I came out with all got HIV, and I feel like there was no way in escaping it, so I might as well enjoy it along the way. No, I don't want to be sick. I guess I just like dick.

The first visit to the doctor had to be the worst waiting experience in my life. They brought me into the office and made me wait. Then, they asked all of these questions about what you like to do in the bed, and who you like to do it with. After finishing what seemed like a therapy session, they finally did a swab test. Then, I had to wait another fifteen minutes before this young white queen came in, and told me that I am reactive to HIV. Then suggests that I find an infectious disease doctor so I can get blood work to know my status for sure. This is some bullshit!

I stormed out that bitch with an attitude. As I walked back to my momma car, my knees started to get weak, my palms were getting all wet, and I couldn't breathe. My big ass fell in the parking lot. It took three white women to pick me up and get me back to the car. White people are overly friendly in the suburbs, and they kept trying to get me to go to the hospital. I kept refusing. Hell, I knew what was wrong with me! Bitch, I just found out my ass was dying. No need to put me in the back of an ambulance for that.

So, all week I've been going over shit in my head after I had lab work done before my results appointment. I was thinking the rapid test could have bene wrong, or that I would be a lucky bitch and escape the HIV epidemic, despite my ways. In reality, today, my life was changed forever. The doctor came in and gave me good news, and bad news. When I heard it, my ass fell down to the floor again. Hell, I had more bruises on my knees from falling this week than from giving head in the park all year.

I had to wait for hours for ultrasounds, scans, and blood tests to come back before he brought his ass back to speak to me. He basically told me my weight loss was due to something else, and that I was bleeding internally. He said he was running tests for possible lymphoma cancer; you know, the blood cancer.

He gave me a while to process that information before he dropped the bomb that I was indeed HIV positive, and very far along the spectrum. In other words; AIDS. He wanted to talk about my sexual practices, but all I could think about was dying. I have never been scared of death before, but knowing I was much closer was mind-blowing. I know it was my own fault, though.

I let guys fuck me without a condom because I wanted them to be pleased, but I also did it for my own pleasure. I usually did things for guys their own man wouldn't do, and I enjoyed that. When you're as fat as I am, you have to do extra things to keep the boys coming back. I have always wondered if I was HIV positive, but I was always too scared to get tested, and now I know why. This is some devastating news.

They're always talking about knowing your status, but the true challenge is what you're going to do once you know? What's next? Where is the commercial telling me not to kill myself, or the commercial letting me know that I can still live? "Wrap it Up" and "Know Your Status" campaigns are some of the most failed campaigns when it comes to actually eliminating HIV amongst black gays. And to think, they get billions of dollars to promote that shit. I just want to know the real reason why they can't find a cure for this shit, and why a virus that was originally a white man's virus became a plague for us black motherfuckers?

"Okay girl, let me know what's going on with you. Why you being so suspenseful? I ain't heard from you all week," Jay Jay says.

"Girls, some stuff about lymphoma cancer, and thyroid issues causing me to lose weight," I add.

"Oh no, that sounds serious! Are you okay?" asks Jay Jay

"Yeah, I am good. The doctor says once more tests comes back to confirm his diagnosis, chemotherapy is a must."

"Wow, well girl, I hope all is well with that! Of course, I am here for you. At least we can shut down these girls saying you got HIV. People always trying to read somebody about their health. Just tacky."

"Actually, I got HIV, too! Bitch, I actually got AIDS," I interject, trying to hold back my tears over the phone.

"Oh my God, Robert! I am so sorry, bitch! I can't believe the doctor told you all that shit today. Are you sure you okay?"

"Yeah, I'm okay. I actually found about the AIDS last week from a rapid test."

"Bitch, I'm on my way to your momma house."

"Naw, I am good. I don't think I can really deal with company right now. I just want to lay in the bed and go to sleep. Sleep my life away."

"Don't act like that, Robert. I know you're going through it, but there's no need to be by yourself."

"Yes, it is. I just got to chill and process this shit. Plus, this medicine they gave me is giving me diarrhea."

"Damn sis, I heard that HIV medicine be fucking people stomach up at first."

"Yeah, last night, I thought I was about to die. I was sweating all night in my sleep, and my stomach had the worse pains I've ever felt before. I just wanted to lay here, and go to sleep. I'm still laying here feeling like I just gave birth."

"What pills are you taking?"

"Something called Truvada."

"Damn girl, this is just too much. I would have had to smoke me a blunt to deal with all that, and you know I only do white women drugs."

"Drugs are the furthest things from my mind."

"I guess girl, it's what I need to survive."

"Girl, you don't need that shit to survive. You just like the way it feels."

"Yeah, but these damn pills be wearing me out! I took a pill a few days ago and didn't go to sleep for two days. I cleaned this whole house up from top to bottom."

"Bitch, you better clean!"

"I know, right? Are you coming out for pride next weekend?"

"Of course I'm coming out for pride! I wouldn't miss that for nothing!"

"Alight, well let me know what plans you thinking of. You know pride is really the beginning of the summer, and plus, I think we need this! We haven't all been together in a while, and it seems like a lot is going on."

"That's true. I need to let my hair down, and have a good time. I'll keep you updated on what's going with me."

"Okay, sis! I'm here for you, girl. Let me know boo!"

Jay Jay always knows what to say make me feel better, even when he ain't really saying much of anything at all. He told me a long time ago that he knew we would be best friends because I made him laugh. I knew we would be best friends the first day we met in class because this bitch called me a girl. Before him, I had never been called a girl before, and I liked when he called me out on my shit. It was like he knew I was one of the girls before I even knew.

We always needed each other to take the next steps in our lives. We both came out to her mommas on the same day. We had been planning that shit in school the whole day, and we were looking up hotel rooms, just in case we got put out. My mom cried, and then hugged and kissed me when I told her, but Jay Jay's mom actually did put him out. That woman is crazy! He had to live with us for a week before his mom allowed him to go back home. They have the most bizarre mother and son relationship.

Trayvon

Summer Summer Summer Time is here. Pride is a national holiday for us. Well actually, black pride *is* our national holiday. And yes, there is a big difference between the white pride and the back pride. We usually use white pride as an excuse to go to the white clubs in the suburbs. On the other hand, black pride is an all-out affair.

It's official pride name is "Hotter than July." During this weekend, you would have all the good clubs open, and parties to go to, most likely at the tangent gallery. These clubs bring in big name celebrities to host their events to make sure the girls come out. This year, Ashanti is hosting the main event on Saturday night. You would also have the Detroit Awards Ball, which is the ball where we would have ball walkers from New York, Atlanta, Ohio, and Chicago (which is only four hours away and they come to town to slay).

Then, we have Palmer Park poppin' all weekend long. Every major city has a designated park for the gays, and Palmer Park was ours. The plan is always to get to the park around three on Saturdays, after spending all day going to the malls, getting haircuts, or creating our outfits.

The corner liquor store is always the first destination; getting two half-gallons of Bacardi Light rum, orange juice, ice, and big red cups. I always love Pride weekend. It's a sense of brotherhood amongst us to celebrate, and have a good time in being gay. Pride is better than Thanksgiving dinner with my family because these guys are my family. I feel more comfortable around them, than I do with my real family.

When you read about the marches and riots in San Francisco on Castro Street, or in Greenwich Village in New York, and the history of what pride means, you feel like you're connected to the struggle of being gay. Being gay and black in parades and festivals now, is only possible because of those who fought before us. Nowadays, most people, including myself, are more interested in the party aspect of pride. I try to make sure that I, at least, stay aware of the importance and value the legacy.

This afternoon, as we approached the park, I could hear house music blasting from the hundreds of cars that were lined up throughout the park. The guys were walking around with their liquor cups and booty shorts. Towards the back of the park, there were girls competing in a j-setting competition, and the older girls were at a table playing spades.

The older girls were always playing cards, and they usually were the only ones actually barbecuing at the park. This particular Saturday, Robert picked me up in his momma's new drop top. He always liked using his momma's cars to come up to the park to stunt in front of everybody, especially with his new skinny body. We found a good place to park in the midst of the crowd, and we started making our cocktails.

"Girl, I can't believe you think Whitney sings better than Mariah," said Robert.

"I didn't say that! I'm just saying that Whitney is widely regarded as being the voice!"

"Bitch, please! Mariah Carey is the voice! Whitney needs to get off that crack before she can come for Motha!"

"Listen, I'm not going to argue over Whitney and Mariah Carey. Whitney is Jay Jay's girl. You know Brandy is my favorite singer," I add as I started sipping on my cocktail.

"Girl, you are crazy. Brandy's voice is horrible. She sounds like she's chewing on cement," Robert said.

"Please, she is the vocal bible, and where did Jay Jay have to pick up Eman from? It's taking them forever to get here."

"St. John's Hospital on the eastside. I think he was up there visiting his momma."

"I feel so sad for him."

"Girl, who you telling? I wouldn't know what to do without my momma. Bitch, I would give a sickening drag performance at the funeral."

"OMG! Bitch, we gone be bringing you dollars at the alter."

"Yes, Bitch! Is that your boyfriend, Eman and Jay Jay walking this way?"

"Eman is not my boyfriend."

"Whatever! I'm glad you guys are finally getting over y'all issues, though."

"I had to just let it go. I got too much going on to be going back and forth with that boy. Everybody knows he a hoe!"

"Stop it!"

"Okay, bitch. And yes, that is them," says Robert as Jay Jay and Eman approached us while we watched the shirtless boys walk by.

"Hey, y'all," Eman says.

"Hey Eman, where you been? I missed you," I add.

After spending that night in the room with Emmanuel a while back, it's safe to say that I am even more in love with this. He held me all night in his bed, and I was on cloud nine. Then, he flipped me over and ate my ass out for hours. I almost died because it felt so good.

Now, I am nowhere near a virgin, but I am not as experienced as Eman. He gently touched my body in ways I have never been touched. He began slowly taking my clothes off, and had me on a euphoric high. I can definitely see what all the hype is about with him. I just worry that that new feelings for him will mess up the friendship we have.

"I miss you, too, bff. I've just been busy with my mom, and figuring out where I'm going to live. She won't be getting out the hospital, according to the doctors. So, we're preparing everything for that. I just stopped paying the rent on the house since she won't be going back. We have been looking for hospice all morning," says Eman

"Man, I'm so sorry to hear that," says Robert.

"It's all good, we saw it coming. I just got my ad back up and running, and I reached out to a few old clients of mine, so I should be able to afford an apartment off Jefferson in a few weeks", Eman adds

"Be careful, Eman, please!" I say fighting back tears.
I just didn't want Eman going back to prostituting. I heard about
what happens to us when we do that, and I would be crushed if
anything happened to him. I want him to make love to me, and not
those nasty dudes who have to pay for sex.

"I will be, Tray. Now, give me some sugar, Sugar," jokes
Eman as he reaches in to give me the biggest kiss on my lips. My
dick became hard immediately.

"Stop it, boy."

"Whatever, you know you like it. Robert, you have really
lost a lot of weight, girl. You must be living in that gym," says
Eman.

"Yes, girl. I only eat broccoli and asparagus, like white
cunts," Robert said.

"Bitch, I made some asparagus the other day, and my
momma had the nerve to say it was crunchy. I told her ass that
her wig was crunchy," Jay Jay said.

"You know your momma love her wigs," added Eman as he
starts to make him and Jay Jay a drink.

"I don't need any wigs, my hair touches my ass, and its all
natural."

"Whatever, Jay Jay! You know you using some of that special cream on your face, and in your hair so it can grow. Damn, I'm
feeling my drink already. I'm so ready to have a good time today. I
need this," says Eman.

"Girl, don't no cream get in my hair. I swallow it."

"Now, that's a man I wouldn't mind swallowing right
there," interjects Robert as he is pointing to this very light-
skinned, cute boy walking by."

"He too light-skinned for me. You know I love the chocolate boys. A'int that right, Tray?" Eman adds.

"Girl, light-skinned, dark-skinned, it don't matter. Do you
see his dick print in those basketball shorts?"

"The real question is; why he out here in those dingy shorts, dirty socks, and old ass flip flops? I mean, he is a cute dude, but he got a hole in his wife beater," I added.

"Girl, you worried about the wrong thangs. All you need to do is put that boy in the bath tub, clean him up a bit, and bitch, he is husband material!

"Bitch, he riding a bike. I doubt he's husband material."

"Miss thang, don't you catch the bus?"

"And your point? I catch the bus to school. I don't catch the damn bus to the park."

"Bitch, let that man live his life! Did y'all hear Lil' Kim is going to be at the Tangent Gallery tonight?"

"Lets do a toast for pride. Raise your cups, bitches," Jay Jay demands.

" YaYa Sisterhood!"

"Yaya!"

With pride being an all-day event, at some point, you have to go home and get ready for the evening affairs. That includes a detailed shower, where you also make sure to use an enema in your butt. Think about it, if you plan on being in the club grinding on good looking dudes all night, taking ecstasy pills, drinking liquor, and smoking blunts, you never know where the night may end up. So, you gotta be always already to have sex, even if you don't end up having sex.

A lot of times when you have drunk sex, it's not planned. Usually, I only get head. I don't mind getting head anywhere. The club, the car, outside the club, your house, the park, wherever, but my friends will fuck anywhere. I've seen Eman fuck a boy at plenty of house parties before. Jay Jay is infamous for a car fuck, and Robert; let's just say with him, there is no limit. So, if there's a possibility you would get fucked, you should make sure you're cleaned out. The last thing you want to do is have an incident where you shit on someone's penis because the word will spread really fast. No one wants to have the reputation of being a shitty kitty.

I like to use an enema just to feel clean. I never would plan on getting fucked after any club, or event, that's just not my thing. Like I said, getting head is just easier for the situation. I'm no lame, but I really like going out to have fun, not sleep with all of Detroit.

Tonight is the all-black party, and Robert is outside blowing his horn for me to come out.

"Can you tell your friends not to be blowing that loud horn in front of my building? This is a senior citizen community," yells my great grandmother as I walked out of the door to get in the car with Robert.

"GeGe said don't be blowing this horn in front of her building, it's a senior citizen community," I said as I got in the car.

"Girl, tell GeGe to come out here and make her a drank, so she can chill out, hunny. Anyway, look who decided to hang with us tonight," adds Robert.

"Hey, Steven. What's up with you? I haven't seen you in a while," I said.

"I know Trayvon, it has been a while. You always act funny with me. I've been trying to get at you, little fella," says Steven while he started to massage my shoulders from the back seat.

"Whatever."

"Girl, we already made you a drink. Hurry up and drink so you can catch up with us," says Robert as he hands me a cup.

Jay Jay

The quickest way to make me mad, is to move my shit without asking me. I specifically had a bag of coke in my pants from the club on Friday, and now I see my pants folded up in a laundry basket. Damn, she gets on my nerves! I am a grown man, and if I wanted to wash my clothes, I would have. Why did she feel the need to come in the basement and mess with my stuff? She is just so controlling!

Ever since my daddy left her when I was five, she has constantly been treating me like I'm her man. I have to get the hell of out this house! I moved to the basement when I was fifteen years old to get some privacy, but she always finds a way to be down here. This is my personal space! When I have boys over, she starts walking all hard so somebody can know she's is in the building.

Girl, they ain't here to see you, so why are you trying to get attention from my dates? I am the only girl they are here to see. Sometimes, she gets drunk and tries to make her way down here to hang with me and my friends, putting on shows and stunts. She is so embarrassing. She knows we don't get along like that, and again, they are not here to see her. They are here to see me.

I've tried to get here make friends and go on dates, but she refuse to buy better wigs and spruce herself up. I told her that don't no man want an old hag.

"Ma," I yell up the staircase while Trayvon was sitting in the basement with me downloading music from LimeWire.

"What is it, James?"

"Why in the hell did you come down here and wash my pants?"

"Who in the hell are you talking to boy, girl, or whatever you are? This is my house, and I do what the fuck I want! You better be glad I cleaned up that stankin' ass room."

"Stay out of my stuff!"

"Shut up before I embarrass you in front of your friends, and turn down that damn music! All that bass is shaking the floor, and I'm trying to watch TV.

"She pisses me off," I whisper as I head back to the computer with Trayvon.

"You two are funny to me. Y'all act like husband and wife."

"She thinks I'm her man, but she needs to go find one."

"When you plan on moving anyway? Robert was telling me you moving to Atlanta."

"Yeah, I'm just waiting on my acceptance letter from the Atlanta School of Design. I actually found me a new boo thang from down there on Black planet. He is fine, bitch. Look at this pic, he got 11 inches."

" Damn, that thing is too big. I wouldn't be able to take all that."

"Girl, please. You just took Steven's big dick the other night at pride."

"What are you talking about?" Trayvon asked looking like he had no clue as to what I was talking about.

"The other night, before the club, with you and Steven in Robert's car," I add.

"Huh? I mean, I was fucked up. I probably gave him some head, but I didn't take no dick."

"Are you sure? I talked to Robert last night, and he gave me details about Steven fucking you in the back seat of his truck."

"What? I don't remember that. Actually, I don't remember much after I got into Robert's car. It was like I blacked out."

"Girl, of course you blacked out. You took two pills."

"Ok, now I'm confused."

"I was on the phone with Robert when he picked you up before the club, and he said him and Steven was going to get you high off two pills, and see how freaky you get."

"What the fuck? Why would Robert do that?"

"Don't ask me, I thought you knew about it."

"Hell naw! You think I would let Steven fuck me?"

"Y'all have messed around before."

"Yeah, we have, but that was just sucking and licking. This makes sense now, I was bleeding yesterday, and I didn't know why."

"Really, Tray? I didn't know you didn't know. You were passed out at the club in the car. I don't even think you made it inside the club. Y'all got there real late, and when Steven and him got to the club, he said you was fucked up in the car. Eman went out and checked on you, and he fell asleep in the car with you."

"Jay Jay, that boy raped me! I would have never let that queen climb my back. Why would Robert set me up to get fucked by Steven? I thought he was my friend, that's some low shit!"

"I'm at a loss for words. Maybe he was messed up, too, and didn't know what he was doing. Just talk to him before you jump to any conclusions," I said calmly trying to calm Trayvon down.

"Can you please take me home?"

"Yeah girl, let me go ask my momma for her keys."

I don't know what in the hell Robert was thinking about setting Travyon up like that. I know these things might happen in the gay community quite often, but we try not to be as messy as everyone else. This situation is bound to blow up, and I will be caught in the middle. Robert seems to be the one starting all the drama in the group with his insecurities, but he is the one with the most issues. He is getting skinnier by the day, and if the wind blows too hard, he will fall over. I'm not saying he deserves what he is going through, but it does seem like he should change some of his behaviors. If we can't rely on protection from each other, then who the hell are we supposed to rely on?

"James," yells my mom from upstairs.

"Yes, lady."

"You gone have to get the hell out my house."

"What are you talking about?"

"You're bringing drugs into my house! This ain't no trap house."

"I'm not bringing any drugs in the house, ma."

"I just asked your uncle about this little baggy that was laying on the laundry room floor. I ain't doing coke, James, so it must be yours. You gotta go!"

"Why the hell you going through my stuff anyway?"

"It don't matter, why are you doing coke and pills all the time? What the hell is wrong with you? Your ass is a druggie and you can't stay here. Hurry up and take your ass to Atlanta, so I can have some peace! Walking around like you a damn girl. You ain't no damn girl. Fucking fag."

"Bitch, who you are talking to? If you wasn't my momma, I would be dragging your ass all across that basement."

"Come on ,then nigga! Do it! You bad. You think you a woman like me, bring it little bitch!"

"I don't want to hurt your old, drunk ass! Now, get the fuck out my face, ma!"

"Get the hell out my house, NOW!"

"Gladly! I can't stand being in this fucking house with your lonely ass!"

"Get the fuck out, now!"

"You are a miserable bitch," I said before she slapped me across the face.

I returned the favor by pushing her down the stairs that lead to the basement. At first, I couldn't believe I pushed her. It wasn't like this was our first fight, she liked putting her hands on me, and getting into this domestic tug of war.

I reported her to my third grade teacher when she punched me in my chest when I talked back to her. We had an open child protective services case for a few years. Every time a case worker would come over, we pretended we had the perfect relationship, but that was nowhere the truth. She always blamed me for my daddy leaving. She would get drunk most nights, and she felt the need to let me know my daddy didn't want no kids, and that I was a mistake.

She told me if she would have found out she was pregnant sooner, she would've aborted me, and he would still be around.

Now that I think about it, she probably never had any more kids thinking he would come back to her. She has been lonely for almost twenty years, waiting for this loser who left her with a child to come back. She was truly pathetic.

It took me all of two minutes before I gathered my stuff, finished off the bag of coke, and called 911 to let them know my momma fell down a flight of stairs.

Trayvon

My body is lost. My mind is lost. My heart feels lost, and I can't really figure out what hurts most in this situation. Am I mad at my friend Robert, who despite my feelings towards him, I have remained loyal to our friendship? I know he has been bitter because I knew he liked me, and I never allowed him to pursue it. I knew he was bitter because a few of the dudes he liked, ended up liking me, and I might have messed around with one or two of them.

I can think of a lot of ways that Robert could be mad at me, all related to boys, but I never knew he was mad like this. I never knew he was so mad, he would allow a man to stick his dick in my ass without my permission. He knows me. He knows I never wanted to have sex with Steven because I have told him that. He also knows that I would never fuck someone in a car in front of him. Robert has to know I would never do any like that.

Am I mad at Steven for being that guy? Being a guy who would take advantage of me when I have always been so nice and friendly to him? I admit we've sucked each other off a few times under really drugged-out situations, but he knew, just like Robert, that I never wanted to have sex with him. Why you might ask? They knew because I told them.

He has asked several times before, and my answer has always been no. Out of all the boys I ever met (besides Eman), I have always been very fond of Steven. I actually kinda liked him at one point. I didn't want to be with him, but I did think he was very attractive. He was a tall, skinny, black boy, who always kept a nice fade, and had very pretty teeth. He dressed like most of the guys in Detroit, with baggy clothes and white tees, but his was more preppy.

He was known to show up anywhere with a du-rag and glossy lips. His perfect blend of masculinity and femininity always caught my attention. Plus, he had a cute little personality, and he was older. On paper, you would think I would have wanted to have sex with him, but I didn't. I am just not interested in getting my number of sex partners so high that I can't count.

He never seemed like he wanted anything from me besides my booty, so I've held out to show him I am more than that. After what happened, I guess I am not. He showed me I wasn't by taking it anyway. I guess I actually ain't more than what he thought I was.

Am I mad at myself? Am I not more than just booty? Am I pretending to be better, or different than the rest of the girls out here? I brag about being so educated, and I get good grades in school, but doesn't that mean I should be smarter with some of the shit I do?

I can't remember a damn thing about what happened to me. All I have is the sore ass, and scar tissue from being plunged by a penis that was too big to go inside of me.   Hell, it could barely fit in my mouth. I blame myself for being out there for these niggas to think I am easy. I like sex and I don't want to be looked at as a prude, but I ain't no hoe. Nobody should being do shit like this to me!

I've been laying this bed all day staring at the ceiling watching old black and white movies. I just finished my favorite movie, "A Star is Born," starring Judy Garland. Judy and I just really connected for some reason.

I don't plan on leaving the apartment today because I feel safe when I am here with GeGe. I haven't told her anything about what happened to me, but I think she can tell something is wrong. She picked up some pound cake and orange sherbet from the grocery store across the street. Then, she made some of her bomb ass macaroni and cheese. She made all my favorites today, and I think it's because she likes when I'm at home.

She always tells me it's not safe out in the streets, and that's the truth! She is at peace when I'm here. She would probably freak out if she found out that her seventeen year-old great grandson was drugged and raped by his friend (and a somewhat crush). Although I am pretty sure she would be able to relate if I told her because all of the women in my family have been raped, or taken advantage of.

Rape in the black community is an ordinary disgrace. My grandmother was raped, my momma was raped, hell, my aunt had grown men jumping out of her window in the middle of the night when she was only twelve. Black women are prey for these predators in most of our families, but now my name is added to that lineage of sexual abuse.

I've gotten my stripes, but like the women in my family, I will press on. I'm not going to let this drama with Steven and Robert break me down. I don't have any words for Steven, but with Robert, I gotta figure out how to find a place to still be friends. I think I can, but I don't really even know.

Eman

I have clearly had enough of Robert's ways. I've tried to mend fences with him and be the bigger person, but now, he's gone too far. How can you do that to Trayvon? That dude doesn't do anything to anybody but try to be a friend to everyone. He's young and innocent, and Robert's old ass should know better. He thinks it's okay to be messy and a queen towards your friends, but fuck that! I'm going to show his ass tonight.

I'm catching the bus to the club to whip his ass. See, I live in far northwest Detroit, and for me to get to the Woodward Nightclub, I have to catch three buses. This is well worth it, though. I've already talked to Steven's stupid ass, and threatened to fuck him up on site. That nigga know not to fuck with me, or any of my friends!

I've told all my house brothers about what they did to Trayvon, and they are going after Steven and Robert, too. I had to come up to the club to confront Robert personally. What the fuck is wrong with him? We have a sisterhood/brotherhood. We know each other's mommas. We be over each other's houses. I mean, we literally hang out together almost every single day. We're supposed to love each other no matter what, you know, protect each other.

I don't care what we say to each other, you don't let your friend get raped in the back seat of your car. Trayvon didn't want to tell me, but I had to drag it out of him. I really couldn't believe the excuses he was making for Robert, but before I got mad, I had to realize that Tray is just young and kind-hearted. He is dealing with things in his way, and I am going to deal with it in mine. I'm going to fuck him up!

As I walked into the club, I saw Robert in the corner with some new girls that he recently started hanging out with (that I don't really care for). I know it's a possibility that if I hit him, they might to try to jump in, but at this point I ain't turning back.

"Let me talk to you for a minute, Robert."

"Girl, what are you doing up here? How did you get here, did you catch the bus?"

"Bitch, don't play with me!"

"Oh really? So, now I'm a bitch? Girl, go find something to do with your life, Miss Thing!"

"Why in the hell would you drug Trayvon so Steven could fuck him?"

"Chile, that is not what happened. He wanted to get fucked."

"That's a lie, Robert. Trayvon said you drugged him!"

"I gave him a pill, like I always do."

"Did he know?"

"No, he didn't. My bad, but hell, I slipped you a pill before, and it wasn't a big deal."

"Well, I didn't wake up with a bloody ass hole! You're sick, man!"

"Bitch, please! Trayvon took the dick. I didn't force him to sit on it."

"But you drugged him, and didn't let him know. If you were a friend, and you saw he was being out of character, you should have stopped it."

"Why would I do that? I wanted to see it."

"You really did set it up, then. You wanted to see them fuck, you fucking pervert!"

"Eman, get the fuck out of my face, and find some dick to suck."

"Suck my nuts," I said as I punched Robert in his nose, making his drink fly out of his hands.

My mind just snapped after feeling several punches coming from every direction hitting my face. Even though Robert hangs out with us all the time, he knows a lot of people in the city. He has been out in the gay scene way longer than we have. Plus, he travels in a lot of different types of social circles, trying to get everybody to be his friend. He especially hangs out with a lot of drag and fem queens, and everyone knows how dangerous they are in Detroit.

Most of them work in prostitution for a living, and many of them have developed strong defensive skills. In other words, they always gotta be ready if some shit goes down. In their line of work, most of them are being brutally murdered, or going missing with their bodies never being found. It's no wonder they are known for pulling blades out of their hair and from underneath their tongue. They're even know for carrying little pistols in their purse.

I held my own, dragging bitches up and down that club. I flipped over several tables, threw chairs, and busted two drag queens over the head with several empty liquor glasses. Then, the security forced me outside into the parking lot. I picked up two orange construction cones, and threw them into the crowd of bitches that were trying to jump me. I followed that up by grabbing a broken stop sign, running into the crowd, and I started hitting girls in the face, making sure I got another piece of Robert.

In Detroit, you have to know how to fight from birth, and not just fight drag queens, you gotta fight everybody. Because of my looks, I've had several gays think I was a weak punk, but I proved myself to be a fighter time after time. I don't fight fair, either. Everything is a possible weapon, and I will do anything to survive a fight. Luckily, Jay Jay came to grab me, and he pushed me into the car before the police jumped out to of their cars spraying mace in everyone's face.

"Didn't I tell you not to come up here? That's why I said I wasn't going to give you a ride," Jay Jay said.

"Listen, I don't want to hear that shit! Your ass should have been up here kicking his ass, too. I'm going to get those bitches back for jumping me."

"Let it go. You already did enough."

"That was just the beginning. I'm going to beat Robert's ass every time I see him."

"Eman, you are right, and Robert was wrong, but he has a lot of stuff going on with him. Maybe that's why he so careless with Trayvon."

"Are you serious, man? There is never a reason to allow someone to rape your friend, and help them do it."

"Robert is sick."

"So what. Half of the city is sick. So, you telling me because you got HIV, that means you can allow someone else to possibly give it to your friend by allowing them to get raped?"

"It's not just HIV, he got AIDS and lymphoma cancer."

"What the hell is that?"

"Hell if I know, but from what his momma said, I don't think he has that much time left."

"Damn! He does look bad, but I don't give a fuck! You just don't do something like that to Trayvon."

"You're right, but hopefully Trayvon will be okay. I know you really love that little boy," Jay Jay added while looking in my eyes for answers.

"Yeah, something like that," I respond, not realizing that I confessed liking Trayvon.

I never thought I would ever really develop feelings for a boy. I remember when I first came out a few years ago, I used to really like this boy in my old neighborhood. He was the finest dude on the block, and we played basketball all of the time after school. This was before I met Jay Jay. I just knew he was gay because of his mannerisms, and how he always wanted to be under me.

He would spend the night over my house, and I would play video games over his house. In my mind, we went together. One day, I told the fucker that I was gay, and he just stopped talking to me. He literally dropped the basketball down on the court, walked away, and never spoke to me again. I would see him walking down the block from time to time after school, and he would cross the street just to avoid running into me. That shit broke my heart. I vowed that day I would never love a nigga again, yet here I am. I love Trayvon.

"Why don't y'all just date, then?"

"Because I don't date, and plus, he is too young to be involved with me."

"But you love him. Eman."

"And so what? You know how this gay shit goes. Love ain't nothing but drama and heartbreak."

"Trust me, I understand. I can't find a man here to save my life. That's why I can't wait to move to Atlanta."

"You be confusing niggas with all that hair. Half of the time they probably don't know if you're a girl or a boy, and you wear girl clothes."

"Well, I can only be who I am. I can't change myself to get a man."

"I'm just saying you would probably get more dudes if you would just man it up a bit."

"Whatever, Eman, that's just your opinion. If a guy can't take me being more feminine, then he ain't the one."

"If you say so, but hey, do you still have some of that spaghetti you made earlier with all twenty different spices and cheeses?"

"Yes, bitch! I do, and it'ss good as hell. Thanks, again, for letting me stay with you. My mom keeps blowing up my phone looking for me."

"Is she okay?"

"Yeah, she alright."

"You know you going to hell, right?"

"Why would you say that? She started it."

"I'm not even going there with you, Jay Jay. You are crazy as hell for pushing your momma down a flight of stairs."

"Says the man who tore down the street sign for a fight."

"It was already broken," I laughed.

As we get into the car and turn down the street the club is on, I can see everyone who was involved in the fight is still standing outside the club. I begin to get angry all over again. My face starts to get really warm and sore from all of the hits I had to take. I felt tears begin to roll down my eyes. I was so hurt for Travyon that I could literally feel his pain. I rolled down my window and began yelling at the top of my lungs,

"You wrong, Robert. Tray is your sister. He still a baby. You wrong, Robert! It ain't over!"

Robert

So the inevitable happened. Eman and I got into a fight.
For years, I have tried to avoid getting physical with him, or anybody. He attacked me at the club, so he deserved to get jumped. I
can't believe he was acting like a fucking maniac. He hit me right
in my face with a Grand Boulevard street sign. He is so ghetto and
classless. Always has been, and always will be.

I know why he's mad, though. I didn't mean for the sex between Trayvon and Steven to happen. I was fucked up, and I let it
happen. I guess part of me wanted to see it, and it was hot. I still
don't think Travyon didn't do anything that he didn't want to do,
but I did slip a pill into his drink. Jay Jay didn't have to run his big
mouth and tell him. Jay Jay even had the nerve to help Eman when
we were fighting.

I know Eman is letting him stay with him at that stunted
apartment, but that doesn't mean he needed to betray me. We
have been friends since high school, but he just met Travyon and
Eman a few years ago. Fuck those bitches! I am officially done
with the Ya-Ya sisterhood. They are no longer friends of mine. The
issue was really a misunderstanding between Trayvon and I, but
Eman is his protector.

Lately, I ain't been hanging with those so-called friends of
mine. I feel betrayed by them. I have given them money, rides,
priceless advice, and guidance. I know I have been a great friend.
By no means am I saying I'm perfect, but I know I'm not a bad person.

Now, I'm in the hospital feeling like death. I've been here
all week, and don't know when they're letting me go home. Sometimes, I feel like it would be better if I just died. I've already lost
my youth.

"Robert, how are you feeling today?" asks the nurse as she
entered my hospital room.

"I'm alright, I guess. When can I go home?"

"I don't know, Robert. That is all up to the doctor, I can't make those kind of decisions. Are your mom, sister, and nephew visiting today?"

"Nah, I told them to stay home today. I feel bad for having them up here everyday. They need a break."

"Can I ask a question?," the nurse asks as she checks my IV.

"Go head, what's up?"

"Where is your father?"

"Ha! Are you serious," I laugh.

"Well, yeah. I always see your mom, but I never your father. Why hasn't your father visited?"

"Are your mother and father still together?"

"Yes, they have been married for twenty-two years."

"Wow, that's beautiful! Well, I don't even know who my father is. Never met the man. I've heard stories about him, maybe saw a picture or two."

"I'm sorry I didn't know."

"Its okay. Most of the black gay boys don't have a father around. Now that I think about it, all of my friends are fatherless."

"Robert, that's really deep. Who teaches you guys how to be men? Who protects you?"

"Nobody. I learned how to be a man out here in these streets. My momma did the best she could with what she knew, and no one protects us. If I had a father, maybe my cousin would not have put his big dick in my mouth at thirteen years old."

"What?"

"Yeah. My cousin, who is straight and married with kids, used to make me suck his penis when I was younger. It happened for years."

"Robert, that is child molestation."

"Girl, he was a child, too. Plus, he is family, and you always have to protect family. My mother said it was just boys being boys. I always wondered though, how he was able to move along with his life as a straight man, and I ended up in this hospital bed at twenty-four with AIDS. God is a trip!"

"Robert, can I pray for you?"

"Chile, yes. I can take all the prayer I can get."

"Grab my hand, and bow your head. Dear heavenly father," she said as her prayer took me to Jerusalem and back. Lord knows I needed that.

Half-way through the prayer, my doctor finally walked in. I have been waiting on this man for the past two days to come in and tell me what the hell is going on. I just don't understand why they keep me waiting so long. I've been so scared, I've thought about killing myself twice in these past two days. I have never thought about suicide before my diagnosis, but with everything that's going on, I just think it would be the easiest thing to do. I am just truly tired of living.

"Hello doctor, I was just praying with our strong patient. It was at his request," says the nurse who is still a bit startled from the doctor entering the room.

"No problem, a little prayer never hurt anybody. How is our patient feeling today?"

"I feel fine, Dr. Kuwura."

"So, the pain in your abdominal area is manageable?"

"Yes sir, the meds have been working. I felt like I was going to die when I first got in here. What is going on?"

"Well according to the CT scan, it looks like your lymphocytes are growing, and spreading throughout your body. We are now entering stage IV of your diagnosis, and it seems it has specifically spread to your central nervous system."

"So, I am dying sooner than expected?"

"Let's not look at it like that, young man. Let's look it at like we have a unique opportunity to come up with solutions to treat you so you can have a comfortable life."

"Dying ain't comfortable."

"We will try to make it as comfortable as possible. Have you continued to take your anti-retroviral drugs since the last time we saw you?"

"Yeah, but I have missed a day or two... here and there. I am not used to taking pills everyday."

"Okay young man, so we have decided that we are going to do another round of chemotherapy, starting tomorrow."

"No! I hate chemo, and I don't want to carry that bag around. It's so embarrassing."

"It's either that, or you will have to come in everyday for your treatment. I thought you wanted to go home."

"I do."

"Well, that bag isn't that bad young man. Remember, our goal is to make sure you stay comfortable during this process, and chemo will help slow the progression down"

"I told you, dying ain't comfortable, doc!"

Eventually, I finally got to go home. I thought I would be excited, but I wasn't. They had to roll me out the hospital in a wheelchair because I was too weak to walk from my room, to my mom's car. We stopped at the Save-a-Lot for groceries on the way home, and I broke down in the parking lot when I got out of the car.

I didn't want to walk into the store and have everyone stare at me with a chemo bag strapped across my body. The machine is so loud, and every sixty seconds it makes this weird noise. If I am standing next to someone, it always catches their attention and they begin to stare at the chemo bag, trying to figure out what it is. I am just not comfortable being looked at as the weak little victim. I am sick, but every morning I wake up hoping this was all just a bad dream, and I go back to my old life of fabulousness.

I want to go back to the life where I worked a good job, made good money, and had girlfriends. The life before I decided to act on the feelings about men I had all my life. The life before I met Jay Jay in the ninth grade. The life I had before I got on my knees and sucked the first boy's cock in the back of the public library.

I didn't have gay parents, nor older friends I could speak to for guidance when I came out almost a decade ago. I linked up with Jay Jay and immediately hit the ground running. I was in the closet when I first started messing with boys. I would create fake profiles on the internet. I didn't want my family to find out, and start acting weirded out.

My mother thought all gays were pedophiles back then, and I didn't want her thinking that about me, especially after my sister had my niece. It wasn't until I met another down-low man that I thought I was in love with. I think his name was Mark, yeah, it was Mark. He broke my heart, and that broken heart lead me to these streets looking for something from these niggas.

Ironically, I never found love, or anything close. I did, however, find a community that loved my jokes and personality. They embraced me being a big girl, and I was free to vogue, and just be myself. I found friends like Tray and Eman. I found a purpose. Now, all I got is this chemo bag, and a few months to live.

Trayvon

So, senior year is moving quickly, and I have to submit all of these applications by December if I want to get into a good university. Going to college is not an option for me. I've been college bound since middle school, and I can't let my grandmother, or the rest of my family, down. Many people think because I'm in the gay scene, I don't have dreams, but that is the furthest thing from the truth.

I want to be a lawyer, and I know I can make it happen. I might stay at the clubs all night, but I take my black ass to school. If I go out of town to walk a ball, I make sure everyone knows I need to be back by Monday morning for class. My friends are very supportive in making sure I stay on track, especially Eman. He always tells me to make sure I keep my grades up so I can get into a good college. I'm not the straight "A" student that I used to be, but I still do fairly well.

"I don't even know why you would fill out a college application for a school in Indiana. What the hell is in Indiana, bitch?" asks Jay Jay.

"Girl, I went on a campus tour last year, and I have a great chance to get a full scholarship," I said.

"Don't listen to this girl. You can apply wherever you want to. You're trying to make sure you have money to get that degree. Hell, it's been almost a year since I graduated, and I'm still working on school applications," Eman interrupts.

"Make sure you apply to a school in Atlanta so you can come down with us next year," says Jay Jay.

"I applied to Morehouse and Clark Atlanta. I'm still on the fence about wanting to go to an HBCU. I've spent seventeen years around black folks, I'm thinking I may need to experience being around white people," I add.

"That's true, diversity is key, hunny," says Jay Jay.

"Thanks for letting me use your laptop. I didn't feel like sitting at that Wayne State University library all day writing these damn essays. I probably would get distracted by being on Black Planet," I say.

"No problem, Tray, enjoy it. I had to fuck two old white men for that laptop," Eman says with a smile on his face.

"Well, you need to fuck two more white men to get some heat in this damn place. It's cold as fuck in here! I feel like I'm typing in the middle of Antarctica," I jokingly say.

"Listen, I barely made enough money to pay rent and keep the lights on this month. I haven't been able to get many clients with the back and forth with mom's chemo treatment. Hopefully, I get the heat turned on, and get some furniture so we can get off this damn floor," says Eman.

"Girl, stop complaining, it's the middle of November. Why don't you get closer to that space heater with your bougie ass. Anyway, I'm heading back on the road driving again. I'm just waiting to pass my drug test, and we'll be all good, Eman," says Jay Jay.

"I don't know about you getting back on the road again if we're waiting on you to pass a drug test. You a pill away from being a crack head, as many drugs as you do," laughs Eman.

"Bitch, I've been clean for two weeks, and I've been drinking hella water and cranberry juice. Hell, I've been too broke to get any drugs," Jay Jay adds.

"Girl, you need a lot more than that," I jokingly add.

"Y'all are so stupid. Let's go to the store and get us another bottle. I'm ready to get loose tonight," Eman said.

"Okay, I'm ready!"

"Let me grab my mink coat," adds Jay Jay as he grabs his coat, and we head down the stairs to the store.

"Has anyone heard from Robert?"

"His little sister called me a few weeks ago, and told me that he was back in the hospital. He doesn't answer the phone when I call. I guess he's beefed out with me, too," Jay Jay tells us.

"Why do you even care, Trayvon? Don't you hate him?"

"I don't hate him. He didn't know better, so he couldn't do better. I am cool with it, now. I mean, we will never be best friends, but I'm over it."

"Fuck that, I hate him," Eman shouts out as we enter the corner liquor store.

"You don't hate anyone, Eman. The boy is dying, shut up," says Jay Jay.

"Shut up with that damn fake fur, and go grab some orange juice from the cooler."

"Bitch, this is my momma's fur. Its real," said Jay Jay as he headed towards the back of the liquor store for orange juice.

As Eman and I walked up to the bulletproof glass window at the counter to order our usual Bacardi Light Rum, three guys walk into the store looking like trouble. They were dressed in black with corn rolled braids, and had their pants were sagging all the way to their knees. They began cursing really loudly, and making a scene as Jay Jay walks up to the counter with his long hair, momma's mink, and thigh high boots.

"Oh hell naw," yells one of the boys.

"This nigga got on a females mink coat, and boots, my nigga," laughs the other one.

"I think these niggas must be some fags!"

"We from Seven Mile, we kill fags on our block."

The Arabic guy at the counter tells us our total was forty dollars. Eman ignores the young black boys, and tells us to give him ten dollars each, and he will cover the rest. I nervously reached into my pocket to give him the ten dollars, and acciden- tally dropped the hundred dollar bill that my great grandmother had given me to get money orders so I could send off my college applications.

I immediately went after the money on the floor, but not after noticing one of the young boys saw it. Eman finished the transaction, grabs the bag, and we headed out of the liquor store. We hadn't even walked ten feet before the boys ran out the store and shot three rounds in the air.

"Empty your pockets, niggas," yells one of the boys.

"Run," screams Eman as he emptied his pockets and darted off.

Bullets began flying left and right. I just kept running at full speed like my life depended on it. I ended up at a dead end, right at the service drive of the I-94 freeway. I could hear the sounds of the fast cars on the freeway below me, and the ground was shaking where I stood. I had no idea what my next move should be. If I jumped over the railing, I would end up in a forest of trees right on the side of the freeway. I didn't know what was down there, or how deep it was. After a few minutes of silence, I thought it was best if I tried to find Eman and Jay Jay before deciding to jump.

"Eman, Jay Jay," I began to yell

"Tray!I see you! Man, you okay?"

"Y'all, I'm over here," Jay Jay hollers as he appears out of an alleyway that leads to the freeway.

"Damn, I thought we was dead," Emans says.

"I literally saw my life flash before my eyes. All I could think about was how my momma was going to kick my ass about her coat. I broke the heel on my boot," says Jay Jay as he tries to catch his breath.

"What was that? Why would he shoot at us like that? He could have killed us," I added, still shaken up.

"That's the point. They don't care, Tray. They wanted to kill us. They probably wouldn't feel anyway about killing three gay guys. They kill people all the time," yells Eman.

"Okay, calm down, Eman. I think the guys are gone, now. Let's walk back to the apartment. We can still have our cocktails. I still have a half a bottle of liquor," whispers Jay Jay, calming the mood.

"My bad, I just feel so helpless," he adds.

"Man, I can definitely use a drink," I say as we walked towards the apartment in complete silence.

I never understood why the straights hate the gays so much. I can remember getting picked on by my cousins when I was younger because I didn't like playing sports. My thoughts are, if it doesn't affect you, why the hell do you care what I am doing with my life?

I had to beat this boy's ass my freshman year in high school for trying to bully me. He thought it was funny to go around the school saying that my breath smelled like nut because I liked to suck dick. The funny thing was, at that time I hadn't done anything sexual with a guy, and I got upset he would spread that rumor.

Usually most of the bullying would happen in fourth period because we shared Chinese class together, and nobody listened to our teacher, Ms. Chang. He got mad at me and my home girl one day because we told him we weren't voting for him for homecoming court. He began to joke about me sucking dick out of nowhere. I politely moved my desk to the side and walked to his desk and punched him right in the face.

We tumbled all over that room. I can still hear Ms. Chang yelling at the top of her lungs for help. I got suspended for three days because of that fight, but he did, too. I played victim, and told the principal about his bullying. I ran into that little jokester at Off Broadway East one night with Robert. Guess I wasn't only one wanting dick in my mouth. It seems the ones with the biggest issues with gay people are the ones that have the biggest issues with themselves.

Robert

Ever since my diagnosis, I've been taking walks, getting some fresh air, and trying to enjoy nature. Between being at home resting ,or at the hospital for treatment, I rarely get a chance just to be outside. I usually come to Belle Isle, off the Detroit River every day at noon, before all the hoodlums and kids skipping school come through with their loud music. It's the time of the year when it's still okay to come outside with a jacket when the sun is at its peak.

The leaves have been turning a nice reddish-orange color and beginning to fall and cover the grass throughout the park. You can see the wind create tides up and down the river as the boats travel through to their destinations. There is so much noise from nature, but at the same time, there's so much peace. Peace that's needed during a very complicated time of my life. And then, there is Canada.

I come here and sit on the same bench and stare across the river at the skyline of Ontario, Canada. I've been to Canada so many times in my life. I mainly went for the amusements park when I was younger, but I went to the casino a lot once I turned 19. You didn't need a passport to cross the Ambassador Bridge back then. Things changed a lot since 9/11.

I often daydream and think about jumping into the river, like the people do on the Golden Gate Bridge in San Fransisco. Maybe all of this would go away if I did. I wonder if I ran away to Canada, and changed my identity, could I live a better life? You would be amazed at all of the crazy shit that runs though my mind.

These days, I'm feeling a lot better, though. The chemo has been working enough for me to finally have enough strength to get out of the house for a little bit. I'm learning to cope with my new life. My family is always so worried about me, and all of the germs that are everywhere. My momma constantly talks about how my immune system isn't strong enough to be hanging out at a public park, but it goes in one ear, and out of the other one.

I had my first drink in what seemed like forever last night. I usually don't drink Hennessy, or any dark liquor, but my taste buds are different now. Things I used to like prior to chemo, I don't like anymore. The smell of rum now makes me sick, so no more Bacardi for me. The liquor burned going down my throat last night, and yeah I shouldn't be drinking, but chile, I got to live!

I've finally gained a little weight, and my face doesn't look so sucked in. I completely stopped going on any dates, or talking to anybody connected to the gay scene over the last few months. I refused to let anyone see me like that, but I look better now. It's not just physical, either. I feel like I am a better person, now. I am happy. Life feels different, and I feel like I'm actually ready to live.

Jay Jay asks to join me at the park every day, and I always tell him no, but today is a brand new day. Yes sir, a brand new day!

"Girl, it took you forever to get here," I yell at Jay Jay.

"Bitch, this damn bench is far as hell from the parking lot. And why are you sitting so close to this water? You ain't thinking about jumping in, are you?"

"Not today, I ain't."

"You so crazy, you look good bitch."

"Thanks, honey!"

"Girl, it's a bit nippy out here. I don't see how you come out here every day."

"The cool breeze makes me feel good, especially when I was on chemo."

"You off chemo?"

"Yeah, for awhile."

"That's a good thing, right?"

"I suppose. Girl, do you remember back in high school, we got a truancy ticket out here for skipping school?"

"Yes, bitch, I do remember that. It was a bunch of us out here. We had just left Coney Island, and we came out here to smoke, and eat our chilly cheese fries."

"Girl, you know I ordered a corn beef sandwich with some wing dings."

"Yes!"

" I was grounded for weeks when my momma found out about that. She said you was bad news, and I should stay away from you."

"Whatever! Your momma had some nerve. You was the oldest one, and the one who had the car that got us out here."

"Yeah, she had no clue what my life was like."

"Neither one of our mommas had any idea. Anyway, you missed the party of all parties, last week."

"Which one?"

"The all-black masquerade party."

"Oh yeah I saw the flyer for that. It was at the Tangent Gallery, right?"

"Yeah."

"Who you go with?"

"Same old girls, Tray and Eman. Of course my gay momma and daddy was there, bitch. It was everything."

"No fights?"

"No, bitch. There were no fights. Everybody was on their best behavior, and we all had good time."

"How's Tray and Eman?"

"They good. Eman's momma is still in the hospital, and he has been dealing with Tray applying for colleges. Bitch, we trying to move to Atlanta in the summer."

" Yass, bitch! Y'all better move to Atlanta."

"You are going, too. It's time for you to make some moves."

"Why would I move down there with y'all, and they still hate me?"

"Chile, they don't hate you, they good. I think the distance has healed the wounds. We are friends, girl. You made a mistake, and as long as Trayvon is good, then it's good. Eman just gone be Eman."

"I guess, honey. I guess I can start showing my face again."

"We miss you."

"I miss y'all bitches, too!"

"But honestly, I do think you should talk to Tray, though. He never wants to talk about it, and I know you hurt him."

"Yeah, I know I gotta make it right. I'll reach out to him."

"That's what I'm talking about, bitch. Teamwork makes the dream work."

"Whatever, bitch. Hold up! Did you hear about that sex party at some mansion with Mayor Kwame?"

"Yes, girl! I did. I told everybody to be careful about voting for that hip-hop mayor. Now he out here spending tax payer's money on hoes."

"Girl, I gagged."

"No, the real gag is GeGe. She practically was his damn campaign manager."

"Right! Trayvon swears up and down that Mayor Kwame is his cousin."

"Lies, honey... lies."

"Let's go over to Greektown and get some Pizza Papallis, I'm hungry."

"Only if we can go to the casino afterwards, I'm feeling lucky."

"Oh, you must got you a coin. Come on girl, let's go."

Jay Jay

Chile, my ass is freezing to death. I just can't take this ghettoness anymore. I am not used to struggling, that is why I haven't ever moved out of my momma's house. I'm the only child, and my mother is retired from the state, so I was raised "middle class." Middle class in Detroit is still below the poverty line in America, but ever since I've moved in with Eman, I feel like I've been living in the projects.

We do not have any heat, no furniture, and we can only eat food warmed up in the microwave. I could have sworn I saw Eman make three packs of ramen noodles in the microwave the other day. What the hell? I'm not going to do that, no matter how hungry I get.

I know I haven't helped the cause because I haven't been on the road driving in a while, but it's all just too much. Earlier, I went to the pay phone and asked my momma if I could temporarily move back in with her. She told me I needed to go by the house so we could talk about it. She was very serious about me not coming back home doing the same thing. At this point, I don't care anymore. Anything has to be better than this. I do love being here for other reasons, though.

Here, I feel a lot more comfortable being myself. I have been wearing a lot of women's clothing, and have gotten in full drag a few times. I know I was against doing drag before, but I think I really like it. I'm just so damn pretty! My girl name is Jazmine Leslie. I actually went to a ball to walk drag, but I didn't get a chance to compete. I was so high, I could barely walk. So, Eman and Tray wouldn't let me walk.

I think I did an eight ball of coke that night, and a bunch of pills. Living the life of Jazmine made for a good night. I might even join a house a little later down the line, who knows? I have always admired the House of Chanel, and all of their female figures. They look so real. I think when I move to Atlanta, I might be Jazmine all the time.

I guess it's time for me to start beating this face since we're going out tonight, and I'm bringing Jazmine with me.

"I see you getting in drag again, huh?" asks Eman as he walked through the front door of the apartment.

"I know what you're going to say, Eman. I need to stop dressing up like a girl, if I don't want to be trans."

"Actually, I wasn't going to say that. You should be able to dress, and be whoever you want to be, without any critique from me."

"Oh ok. Looks who is being a supportive friend," I jokingly said, very surprised by Eman's response.

"What did the trucking company say?"

"They want me to come in on Monday for orientation."

"Oh wow! Man, that's great!"

"Yeah, it is. I'm just hoping this snowstorm they're predicting we are going to get comes and goes before I have to hit the road," I add, wondering when it would be a good time to tell Eman that I was moving back home.

"Yeah, your income will help out a lot. This is my first time on my own, and this shit is hard!"

"Eman, you good. You're doing good for yourself. You're only 19, but hey, I have something to tell you."

"What is it?"

"Never mind. We can talk later," I said feeling for some reason, it wasn't a good time to bring it up.

"Oh, ok. I can wait until you are ready. You know you are really pretty, Jay....I mean Jazmine."

"Ok, cut the shit! What the hell is wrong with you? You come in here being overly nice and shit."

"You don't think I'm nice?"

"Yeah, Eman, I think you are a sweetheart. What's wrong, for real? You seem sad. What's up?"

"She's gone!"

His words were yelled at top of his lungs, seemingly cracking every mirror and glass in the house.

"What? Are you talking about your mother? What are you doing here? How did you get here?"

"Yes, Jay Jay, my momma is dead! I caught the bus here. I couldn't stay at that hospital any longer. I've practically lived there all year, hoping and praying that she would get better, but she didn't. She's gone," cries Eman.

"Brother, come here. I'm sorry to hear that. I love you, man. Your mother is in a better place. She was a beautiful woman," I said as I embraced Eman and hugged him with all the love I had.

"I don't know what to do next."

"Have you told your family?"

"No. After she stopped breathing, I called the doctor, and they pronounced her dead immediately. I just left the hospital!"

"Well, let me get you back to the hospital so you can start taking care of things, and call your family. I'll be here with you every step of the way," I add, as I begin to think of how painful it would be if I lost my mother.
I just thank God I didn't tell him I planned on moving.

The ride down 75N was a quiet one. This year just has been so much for us. It's like shit is happening back-to-back. How much can we take? I sometimes question God, and why he chose us to suffer so much. Life really shouldn't be this hard.

My heart is bleeding for my brother, Eman. While I am the peacemaker of the group, Eman, by far is the strongest. He is our protector. He is the one who would give up his life if anybody tried to hurt any of us, but right now he is hurting. Who has the strength to protect our warrior? Eman fights so hard because he loves so hard. He is just a big soft ball on the inside, and I hope the loss of his mom doesn't turn his heart cold.

By the time I got him back to the hospital, some of his family had made it there. I had never met any of his family before today, and I think I saw his momma once. The one thing I'm noticing immediately, is how dark-skinned his family members are. His aunts and cousins almost look like Africans, and Eman is bright as hell with curly looking hair.

His look is one the reasons he is such a hot commodity in these streets, beside his penis, of course. You know the girls are still caught up in the whole light skin vs dark skin, and most times, light skin wins. Everybody wants a light-skinned nigga, and Eman is the prettiest of them all. I remember him telling us that his daddy was Puerto Rican when I first met him, and he started speaking Spanish.

He told us he learned Spanish and English from his grandparents on his father's side when he was a baby. Now that I think about it, that was probably the only time he ever mentioned his father, or his family. Looking around the lobby of the hospital, I saw that he was definitely the light-skinned, black sheep of the family.

I forget how loud, and how quiet the hospital can be. While there are so many noises and people around, there's also a quiet feeling. It's almost like the feeling of death, and that shit is scary! I don't like it at all, and no matter how much I despised my mother, I wouldn't want her to die. She is a very flawed person, but she's all I have, and without her, I might lose it.

"Can we go home now? My aunt is going to handle the rest of the arraignments," asks Eman walking up to me with tears in his eyes.

"Yes, let's go home"

Trayvon

My mind has been running wild ever since those dudes tried to shoot us at the liquor store. From getting jumped at the club, several robberies, the crazy guy at the bus stop, and even the shoot-out at the ball where the boy was laying helplessly in the middle of the street, I just feel like I'm constantly surrounded by evil spirits. The evil spirits are trying to take me out of this world, and I pray God continues to watch over me.

As I get older, I am slowly realizing life can be taken away from you quickly, and there is nothing you can do about it. So, when Robert reached out to me to discuss the situation with him and Steven, I didn't want to meet up with him to talk about it. I've made my peace with it. Who wants to keep talking about getting raped over and over again?

Eman thinks I'm being weak and letting them get away with it too easily, but I had to tell him not to bring it up again. He is so obsessed with getting revenge from Steve, but after his fight with Robert, I begged him to let it go. I eventually saw Steven agin after it happened, and basically acted like everything was okay. I made it seem as though nothing ever happened, but I just didn't have the nerve to bring it up again.

I played along with him, and decided that day, to never to speak to him again. The situation was embarrassing enough when it happen, there was no need in making it an ongoing, year-long ordeal. I felt the same way about Robert, as well. I haven't seen him much since it all happened, and that distance was satisfying enough. I can't punish him more than what God is already doing to him. From what I hear, he is already getting punished by death. Jay Jay says he ain't doing so well, and even though I don't hate him, I cant say I feel bad for him. You get back from this world, ex- actly what you give.

He wanted to meet up at Eman and Jay Jay's house since he had never been. He wanted to talk to me and Eman, but I didn't tell him that he wasn't going to be here. I know him and Eman not at their best, and since Eman mom's passing, I didn't think it would have been good to have them meet. I should be with Eman, but instead, Robert wanted to talk about what happened. I really wouldn't be entertaining it if it wasn't for Jay Jay's peace-making ass.

"Whaddup, girl? How you doing?" Robert asked as I let him through the front door.

"I'm good, just preparing for graduation. Nothing major."

"That's good. I heard y'all moving to Atlanta next year."

'Yeah, we've been talking about it, but really, it depends on where I decide to go to school. I have to get out of Detroit. I know you heard about those dudes robbing us at the liquor store, right?"

"Yeah, Jay Jay told me about it. These straight dudes is try- ing to murder us."

"Tell me about it. I'm still on edge."

"I would be, too."

"How you been? I know you been going through some health issues."

"Yeah, I've been going through some shit. I had to spend a few days in the crazy hospital."

"Really? For what?"

"Did you know I got HIV and cancer?"

"Yeah I did."

"I figured you did, but basically the shit's been hard for me. I've been in and out of the hospital, in and out of chemo treat- ment, taking ten pills a day. Hell, I just snapped!"

"Snapped? What the hell did you do?"

"Girl, I tried to kill myself! I took a whole bottle of Tylenol 4s."

"Robert, why would you do that?"

"Girl, I just felt like it would be better. I'm depressed all the time. I couldn't go out anymore. All I did was sit in the house, or sit at the damn hospital. I ain't got no friends, beside Jay Jay. You and Eman mad at me, and no nigga want to have sex with my sickly looking ass."

"Me being mad at you is no reason to want to kill yourself, and besides, you knew you might be sick! You told me that all the time, and you still kept having sex with everybody, unprotected."

"Thinking you sick, is a lot different than actually being sick. It's horrible. Sometimes, I feel it's better to die now, and stop prolonging the inevitable," Robert said with tears rolling down his face.

"You gotta fight, Robert. You can beat this! You can live, but you gotta believe," I said as I grabbed a paper towel to wipe his face.

"Yeah, you right, girl! That's what they say at the coo-coo hospital."

"You sure you don't need to go back?" I laughed, tying to to make him feel better.

"I'm sorry, Tray."

"Sorry for what?"

"For asking you to ride with Steven and I, when I knew he wanted to fuck you. For putting a pill in your cocktail, and not telling you. For watching you take another pill, when I saw how out of your mind you were, and not protecting you. For watching you and Steven make out in the back seat of my car, knowing it was going to go further, and not stopping it. For letting Steven pull your pants down and put his dick in you, when I knew you didn't know what was going on. For watching him fuck you in my rearview mirror when you laid there passed out. I'm so sorry, Tray. I am so sorry."

"Oh, wow! That's a blow to the gut. Thanks for telling me what happened. I never knew. I didn't think I wanted to know, but that helped."

"For real, Tray, I hate myself for doing that to you. You didn't deserve that."

"So, why Robert? Why in the hell would you let that happen? I guess deep down I was never really mad at Steven's simple ass, but you, why would you do that to me? I am your friend, Robert. That's fucked up! I am only seventeen years old, and you let him fuck me while I was passed out. Why?" I yelled while I started to get upset.

"I was jealous of you. I was jealous of you and Eman. I was jealous of how you two always have guys wanting y'all, and they never want me. I was jealous of the fact that even though I was your friend first, you chose to fall in love with Eman, knowing I loved you. I wanted you to feel a little of the pain that I carry with me everyday. No one ever loves me back. I knew once you found out what Steven did to you, you would be mad, that's why I told Jay Jay. I knew he would tell you, and I wanted to finally get a chance to see you naked. I've been wanting to see you naked for years. I'm sick, Tray. I'm sick in the head.

"Robert, you know what, man? I can hate you right now, but my heart is really telling me that I can't, knowing what you're going through. I'm mad at myself for not being able to want you to die for your shit, but I love your ass. I love you, Jay Jay, and Eman. You gotta get help, man, and you gotta live. I'd rather learn to forgive you on earth, than to still hate you, and you not be here. It's not worth it. I don't need Steven in my life, but I want a better version of you."

"I'm sorry, Tray. I'm sorry. I am sorry," yells Roberet as he becomes more hysterical than he was before.
My God; my young ass wasn't ready for all this.

Eman

So, where do you find the strength to bury your mother? I've looked high and low for some advice, encouraging words, coping techniques, or anything else that would help me deal with the pain of my heart. My body hurts so bad, it has been hard for me to even get out of bed. I hear people talking to me, but my mind can't process the words. I've tried to eat, but the food evaporates on my tongue, and becomes air. It's like it disappears without bringing my body any nourishment. I've cried so much, I truly believe there are no more tears left in my body. I'm an empty vessel, looking for his next move through this map called life.

Who would have thought I would be standing here giving the eulogy at my mother's funeral? What do I say about her? Do I look into the crowd at this church and let them know my mother was my life? Do I tell them that Leslie Johnson was born November 17, 1968 in Detroit, Michigan to Joseph and Roberta Johnson? Or that she graduated from Wayne State University in 1990 with a degree in Social Work, and that she had worked for Detroit Cares since 1993?

Do I say Leslie welcomed her only child, Emmanuel Johnson, on February 7, 1984? Do I tell them she is survived by her parents, Joseph and Roberta, and her son Emmanuel, as well as her siblings, Larry, Lindon, Laurie, her grandparents, aunts, uncles, nephew, nieces, cousins, and other family and friends? Do I tell them that my mother was a devoted mother, and community organizer? She gave her life helping people and outreaching to provide a better life to the homeless. She loved music and dance, and she was an avid supporter of the arts. She was funny, charismatic, and the nicest person you would over met. What else should I say that's not on this paper? Come on, Eman, let your words flow.

"All I can say to you guys is that I loved my mother. I am glad she is in a better place, so she will no longer suffer from cancer. She is no longer in pain. My mother was my best friend, and I will miss her every day of my life. I know sometimes I come off as guarded, but this hurt me badly and I'm glad I have support from you guys. Without my friends and family, I don't believe I could have survived this. Thanks to all you guys for coming to my mother's funeral. Thank you all so much."

It was truly the hardest thing I ever had to do, but I made it through. The ride to burial site seemed like the longest drive in history. As I sat in the limousine, I stared out of the window, and watched how traffic was stopped for my mother. The city stood still as we carried my mother's casket to where we would lay her to rest. I wasn't just sad about my mother, I was sad that I wasn't doing the things that would make my mother proud.

I needed to come up with a plan to make sure I became all of the things she wanted me to be. I can't have her looking down on me selling my body to pay my rent, or stripping at clubs throughout the city. My momma would probably roll over in her grave if she knew some of the things her son actually did. I have to change some kind of way. I just didn't know how.

After laying my mom to rest, we all headed over to my grandmother's house for the wake, and honestly, I really just wanted to go back to the apartment and get some sleep. As I walked up to the house, I saw Trayvon and Jay Jay standing on the porch with a person I hadn't seen in a while; Robert. Initially, I was in shock when I saw him because we hadn't seen each other since we got into our fight. As I really looked at him, I saw how bad he looked.

Tears began streaming down my face as I went to give him a hug. He looked like my momma did the week before she passed. Despite all the drama we had been through, seeing him made the day better. It reminded me some people are here on earth with the chance to still fight. Life is too short, and sometimes you have to let stuff go to get to a better place. Robert and I needed to find a way to get to that happier place.

"Damn, bitch, this wasn't the greeting I was expecting," Robert said as I let go of my hug I had on him.

"I know, man. I'm just happy to see you. Thank you for coming," I added.

"Are you kidding me, Eman? I couldn't live with myself if I wasn't here to support you. I don't care what we go through, I got you."

"I'm sorry bitch," I said.

"No, girl, I'm sorry for what happened. I'm sorry to you, too Trayvon. I was tripping. I should not have allowed that to happen," cries Robert.

"It's all good, Robert. I forgave you a long time ago," says Trayvon.

"Bitch, your grandma is slaying in that dress, honey," laughs Jay Jay.

"I know, right. I told her it was a little too tight for a funeral," I add, smiling.

"Well, I need to ask her where she be getting her pieces from," jokes Jay Jay.

"Bitch, you dumb."

"How are you feeling, Eman? That was a great eulogy you gave."

"I guess I'm doing as good as I can be. I'm just really glad she is in peace now," I answered.

"I totally understand. Now, let's get in this house and eat. I made the greens, and spaghetti. And let me tell you, I put my foot in it, chile," said Jay Jay as he ushered us into the house to join the rest of the family.
Despite the hurt from losing my mother, I had joy on the inside knowing we were all together again.

I saw a bird, and it reminded me of Ma. I was out on the balcony smoking a blunt this morning, when a bird flew towards me. It landed on the ledge, almost on top of my hand. In all of my life, I never had a bird get close to me and start walking without flying away. The only birds that tried to do that shit are those nasty pigeons that hang around at the bus stops downtown. This bird was beautiful, and unafraid, and I knew it was a sign from

Ma. Ma was telling me to stay strong, and stay beautiful inside and out. That's exactly what I was going to do. I'm going to do it for Ma!

Robert had the idea to go out, so we could both get out of the house. I haven't been out since Ma's funeral, and apparently, he hasn't gone out the whole time he has been doing chemo. The universe is a funny bitch! Who would have thought cancer would bring Robert and I back together? Don't get me wrong, I still have my issues with him, but watching him go through what Ma did, I knew he could use the support from all of us.

He decided we should go to OFF Broadway East to catch the drag shows, and I was down. Even though Trayvon hates drag shows, I actually enjoy watching the performances. It's like an art form, and I love watching them express their creativeness. Going to that club was always Robert and my thing, especially when our favorite performer, Nina Simone St James was headlining.

I was sitting at our table, sipping on my cranberry and vodka I got with my fake I.D., when she hit the stage in the biggest gown I had ever seen. It took four dudes to help her hold up her dress so she could walk out. The lights went dim as I began to hear the music for Regina Belle's *If I Could*. I instantly begin to feel the tears fill my eyes because that was one of Ma's favorite song. Music always brought us together.

I remember her singing this song to me when I was little. As soon as I saw Nina Simone St. James mouth the the words, *"If I could, I"ll protect you from the sadness in your eyes, give you courage in a world of compromise, Yes I would If I could,"* I began smiling. These weren't tears of sadness, but tears of joy because I loved that song. My Ma loved this song! I threw every dollar I had in my pocket onto the stage as she performed.

"You betta do it, bitch! You betta do it!"

Robert

Every year I throw the best Christmas parties. I usually rent a house, and all of us stay here and party all weekend long. I used to try to have parties at hotels, but that never seemed to work out well. Somebody usually called the police because of noise, or because somebody wanted to smoke weed in the hotel of a non-smoking hotel. Stupid fucks!

I usually rented a house way out in the suburbs, isolated from people, and we invited our closest associates and dates to party with us. What goes on at those parties, stays at those parties. It's been known to turn into an orgy, and we like to keep all that info amongst the group.

This year, I decided to add a "trim a tree night" for the first night. I pictured us all exchanging gifts with each other. It would be like our version of "Secret Santa." The first night is always the bonding night where we played games, or cooked our big Christmas dinner.

Two weeks ago, we all drew names out of a bag, and we had to buy a gift under $100. I'm so interested in who got my name. Ever since Eman's mom funeral, we have been in a great place in our friendship, but we've still kept a bit of a distance, and I still had other friends I hung out with.

I wonder what they will give me. I ended up pulling Eman's name out of the bag, and I had no clue what he would want. It literally took me a whole week to figure it out.

"Would y'all be mad if I told y'all I forgot about Secret Santa?" asked Jay Jay.

"What do you mean, you forgot? We have been talking about this for weeks now," I said getting a tad bit upset.

"I know, and I was supposed to get some money from my mom, but I never got the chance to go over there to pick it up. Y'all know I'm broke," Jay Jay explains.

"Bitch, why you didn't say something? I hope your ass didn't pull my name," Eman rudely says.

"No, I didn't, asshole!"

"Well, whose name did you pull?"

"I pulled Trayvon's name."

"How in the hell are you not gonna get him a gift, and it was his idea do to the Secret Santa?" Eman adds.

"It's no big deal, y'all. Go ahead and exchange the gifts, so I can see what y'all got," Trayvon interjects.

"Bitch, don't worry, Tray, I got you. I'm going to get you a fabulous gift next week," says Jay Jay as we began exchanging gifts, and revealing who pulled whose name.

"I guess, girl. So, who did you pull Trayvon?" I asked trying to hide my annoyance with Jay Jay.

He knew this was my night to make up for all the drama I caused all year, and I needed him to pull through. This isn't the first time he has done something like this, though. I mean, I love the girl with every bone in my body, but she has been known for being selfish. She has to learn the world doesn't revolve around her, and it's not always about her needs. He is a sweetheart, true, but chile, the bitch is cheap.

"I pulled Jay Jay's name. How ironic, right? Here you go, girl."

"Aww, thank you sister. I swear I'm going to get your gift. I feel so guilty that I don't even want to open the bag."

"Girl, open the bag so we can see what Tray got you," I interject.

"These are so cute girl, thank you! These are the boots we saw at Fairlane," says Jay Jay as he went to give Jay Jay a hug.

"Those are cute, girl. You betta get her gift! Well, I'm next, and I pulled Eman's name."

"Oh, hell naw! That is so crazy," Eman laughs out.

"I know, but I kept it simple, and got you a cologne set. Here you go, boo."

"My man, thanks Robert! I love the way Paris Hilton smells. I've been wanting a bottle for a while."

"I remembered."

"So, I guess it's obvious I pulled your name. Here you go, bitch," says Eman as he hands me a small envelope.

"Bitch, no way," I yell as I opened the envelope.

What did he get your dramatic ass?" Trayvon asks.

"Bitch, he got me tickets to see Karen Clark at Cobo Hall. I've been trying to get tickets for weeks, but they been sold out. How did you get them?"

"Let's just say I know someone who knows someone, who knows someone, who does Karen and Dorinda's hair."

"Thanks, Eman."

"Ok, ladies, this has been cute, but I need a drink," says Jay Jay, who tries to ignore the fact he was only one who didn't buy a gift.

After our Secret Santa was somewhat of an epic fail, we went straight into playing liquor games. Shady Hearts is one of our favorite games. Basically, we would all get into a circle with a glass of liquor, with no chaser. We place a deck of cards in the center of the circle, and began going around in the circle flipping cards over. If one of us flips over a heart, everyone else asks that person a question. That person then gets to choose what question to answer, and everyone else has to take a shot because your question wasn't the one that got answer.

This card game gets all the juicy tea out. It starts off with very basic questions, but once that liquor starts to kick in, it can lead to arguments and orgies with the right group. This game helps us air out our dirty laundry with each other.

"Bitch, you got a heart," I said as Eman pulled a heart from the deck.

"Oh gosh, I am not ready for this. Go ahead with y'all crazy ass questions."

"Did you actually fuck Larry and his daddy at the same time in a threesome?" I asked.

"Are you really uncircumcised?" Jay Jay asks.

"What kind of dude would you actually settle down with?" Trayvon asks.

"Bitch, that question was boring as fuck! You trying to be all romantic," I said, knowing the game was heading in another direction.

"Whatever, Robert! Just because of that comment, I'm actually going to pick Trayvon's question to answer, so that means you bitches have to take your shots," screams Eman, who was clearly feeling his liquor.

"Damn, y'all never pick my questions. I'm drunk as fuck," Jay Jay stutters out.

"Your question was stupid. Everybody knows my dick is uncircumcised, but who cares nigga? It's big as fuck," Eman says drunkenly.

"So, you going to answer my question, or not nigga?" asks Trayvon.

"Yes, little nigga, I am. Can you give me minute to think? Damn! Let me see. As you know, I'm not the settling down type, but if I did, it would be you, Tray. From your maturity, innocent spirit, and sex appeal, I would want you, little nigga," says Eman grinning from ear-to-ear.

"Oh my God! I told you this game was going to get lovey dovey. That was very beautiful, Eman. I wish you two would just hook up, and get over it. This brother shit is getting old," I added as I made a full cocktail, instead of just the shots.

"Eman ain't ready," says Trayvon, who clearly begins to feel his drink.

"Nigga, what you mean, I aint ready? You can't handle me, boy. Don't let that liquor get your legs in a position that you can't take dick in," Eman said grabbing his dick.

"Yuck, you two are gross, honey. Two girls bumping pussies in the bed," says Jay Jay.

"I ain't got no pussy, bitch! I got ass and dick," says Eman.

As we finished Shady Hearts, we started playing Truth or Dare, and then Scategories. We drank, smoked, and had the best night. And this was only the beginning of our epic Christmas night. No one could have imagined it would have been our last one together, but at that time, it felt good. I missed my bitches.

Trayvon

Tonight is the night I have been waiting the longest for. I basically told Emmanuel, in front of everybody, that I wanted to fuck. I brought all the essential items needed to take his big ol' dick. I brought my enema bottle to make sure I clean myself out properly. I actually had to skip out on the big dinner Jay Jay cooked for this weekend, so I wouldn't have heavy food on my stomach.

I brought the sexiest underwear I owned. They are a pair of thongs I bought from a sex store a while ago, but I've been scared to wear them in front of people. I'm nowhere near a prude, but I usually have a hard time expressing my sexy side. I identify myself as fully versatile. Basically, I like giving dick to the boys, but I like getting dicked down, as well.

Unfortunately, because of my height and dick size, most guys I meet are usually bottoms, and they want me to fuck them. With Emmanuel, all of that is different. When I first met him, I had the biggest crush on him. He was so fine, down-to-earth, and he treated me very well. It was the way he talked to me. I mean, he is masculine, but he is definitely in touch with his feminine side.

We have grown to be best friends, but lately, our connection has gone to another level. From dealing with his mom's death, and Steven basically raping me, we have been there for each other. The one time I spent the night over his mom's house, I thought it was going to go down, but the timing just wasn't right.

I wasn't ready to be clear about what I wanted from him. I love this boy, and yes, he is my best friend, but I want to him to make love to me. I've had sex with other guys since I've known Emmanuel, but every time I'm fucking these dudes, I'm fantasizing about him. He looks at me like I'm young because I'm not as experienced as he is.

He is only a year and a few months older than me, but honestly he has lived a much wilder life than I have. I'm not a kid, though. I can fuck just like him, and I need him to recognize that.

I'll be eighteen in a few months, and I want a relationship. I know having sex with him doesn't guarantee we'll evolve into having a relationship, but I have to step up and take the chance.

So far, this weekend has been a blast. I have been drinking, smoking blunts, and I got an E pill just to spend a blissful night with Eman. The party is off the hook, and Robert blew Vicks Inhaler into my eyes to take my high even higher. People are all over the house. Some are playing spades in the dining area, some are dancing and vogueing in the living room, and some are in the bathroom getting (and giving) head.

It's around 3 AM, and I'm getting so horny, I'm ready to make a move on Eman. Where the hell is he?

"Jay Jay, do you know where Eman is?"

"I think I heard him say he was going upstairs to go to sleep. He is fucked up," he answered.

"Hell, me too! I'm rolling hard off this E pill!"

"Bitch, who you telling? I've take two pills already!"

"Bitch, you are a junkie! I'm going upstairs to find Eman."

"Bye, bitch. And can you please get the dick? Its obviously time for y'all to fuck. Stop stalling."

"Stay out of my business, bitch!" I respond as I start to walk up the stairs to the room that Eman and I were sharing for the weekend.

I walked into the room, and Eman was staring out into the night, with no shirt on, and white Calvin Klein briefs on. My eyes immediately went to the print of his dick that was bulging out of underwear. Eman is really a handsome looking dude. He is clearly mixed with Latino in some capacity, but I never asked how. His mother was clearly a black woman. Maybe his father was Latino, but he never talked about his father.

"Eman, why are staring out of the window?"

"Shit, I'm just high as fuck. Daydreaming. Thinking about my mom, and thinking about my life."

"What about your life?"

"I don't know, really. When I try to think about my life, not much comes to mind. It's kind of scary."

"You will be fine, Eman. Don't worry so much."

"You're right, man. What the hell are you doing up here? Are you having a good time? This party is better than the one we had last year."

"Yeah, this has been an epic weekend! I am feeling so good right now."

"That's just your pill talking."

"Whatever! Did you take a pill?"

"Actually, I didn't. I wasn't in the mood. I just drank, and smoked a couple of blunts. I also had to make sure I kept an eye out for you. You remember what happened the last time Robert gave you a pill."

"I know, but it's different this time. I guess it is because you are here with me. You're always looking out for me."

"Yeah, man. I got you. I can't let shit like that happen to you."

"What if I want it to happen?"

"Huh? What the hell are you talking about?"

"I mean, not like that. What if I was high, and I had sex with the person I want to have sex with?"

"Sounds like a good time for you. Who do you want to have sex with?"

"Come on Emmanuel, stop playing. You know I wanna have sex with you."

"But why, though? Why me? I ain't all that, Tray. You can have any dude you want. I'm trouble, you know what I do. You know what I'm involved in. Go get a wholesome dude who can treat you right."

"Kiss me, Eman!"

"You sure?"

"Yes. I love you, and I want to make love to you, nigga. I want you so bad. I think about you all day long. Kiss me, Eman. I love you!"

Eman grabbed me by the waist, and kissed me for what felt like an eternity. He turned me around, and placed my hands up high against the window, and began kissing my neck and ear lobes. He began pulling my pants down, and exposed the thong I had worn just for him. He smacked me on my ass as he pulled my thong to the side and stuck his tongue in my ass as he got down on his knees.

With my undies around my ankles, he spread my legs as far as they could go, and he made me feel better than I had ever felt before. I felt like I was going to bust from every lick he gave as my ass got wetter and wetter. I stood up and grabbed him by his penis through his Calvin Klein underwear, and began to pull it out. I used it to guide him to the bed.

As I got him on his back I began to lick the tip of what had to be the prettiest dick I had ever seen. It was huge and tasted even better. I tried to go as far as I could down my throat, but I kept gagging. I did my best, never really been all that good in that department. I flipped him over, had his ass in the air, and began to try to give him pleasure like he did me up against the window.

I grabbed a condom out of my book bag, and began rolling the condom down on his shaft. I spit on the dick three times, and sucked it with the condom three more time after lubing my booty up, and sat on the dick. I rode it for a long time enjoying every thrust. I felt his girth get bigger and bigger inside of me. I was looking into his eyes as I was on top, and I saw something that I never seen before.

It was beautiful a moment; being able to see his soul through his eyes. I was making love for the first time to a guy I was madly in love with. He picked me up, and began giving me head before he placed a condom on my dick. The next thing I remember seeing was Eman on all fours, and he whispered in my ear to fuck him.

I slid my dick inside of him, and all of sudden, my pill must have really started to kick in because I began fucking him like a porn star. I started pounding harder and harder, and he began to scream, and the next thing I knew, I was cumming. It was the biggest explosion my body has ever felt. It was literally the best 20 seconds of ass I have ever had. I hope he wasn't mad I nutted so fast, but hell, I couldn't help it.

After falling out on the bed full of sweat, Eman began lying on my chest.

"Let's do this, beautiful," he says.

"Do what?"

"Let's try to do this relationship thing."

"Are you sure? Are you ready?"

"After letting you fuck me like that, I can't imagine thinking of you with another man. I need you. I need to be with you. I'm ready."

"Let's do it, Eman. Let's do it," I add as I began smiling while playing in Eman's hair. I finally got my man.

Jay Jay

So, I am back on the road. Thank God! I knew my ass needed to get back to driving these trucks if I was going to survive in these streets. Once my drug test came back negative a few months ago, I immediately started driving all over the country. I ended up back at my mom's house for a brief moment, but she put me out when she found out I was on hormones, and transitioning into a woman.

I just don't understand why she has to be so jealous of me. She basically made me the woman I am today, and she can't stand that I am just as feminine as she is. She had the nerve to tell me she birthed a son, and she would never accept having a daughter.

So, I packed up my shit, and moved back in with Eman. The only difference in moving in with Eman this time was that Trayvon was over there all of the time. Ever since they started their relationship, our friendship is always based on what they want to do as a couple. It's weird when two people who were a part of a friendship get into a relationship.

All of their good and bad times, are now the concern of everyone else, and it becomes draining. I love me some Eman and Trayvon, but they are a handful sometimes. So, I have been focusing on my transition and getting my paper up, so I can get this apartment in Atlanta in the summer.

I met this guy online last week who also drives trucks, and he likes chicks with dicks. Even though I have started taking my hormones, most people think I am still just a pretty boy. I haven't made too many changes in my everyday life, except when I get in full drag at night. I'm taking my time with the process. I don't want to do too much, too soon. I also don't want to get work done to my body without having the money to get it professionally done.

I won't be letting just anybody pump silicone in my ass, or get my breasts done in someone's basement. I'm going to get my work done in Canada when I can afford it. The guy I met online and I both thought it would be a good idea for us to drive trucks together. That way, we can make more money, and be on the road a lot longer.

Even though I just met him, I wasn't against the idea because I get bored on the road. I rarely made it back to Detroit unless there was an important event going on, or if I just needed a break from working. Plus, I think I really like this guy a lot. He accepts me for me, and he doesn't want me to pretend like I am masculine.

We've been having a good week on the road together. We parked the trailer in an empty lot, and took the truck all over in whatever city we were in. He's always able to find the best drugs, no matter where we are. It was my turn to drive into Sugar Land, TX, and this nigga is already fucked up! He has been taking bumps all afternoon, and entertaining the fuck out of me. Actually, I've also taken a few bumps while driving. I have to admit, I'm a driver great when I am high.

"So, how is it back home in South Carolina? I've never been down there before."

"I mean, it's cool. It's country. I'm a country boy. Much of my life there revolves around my family."

"Does your family know about you?"

"Hell, no! There is no way! We ain't like how you and your people are in Detroit. I would never have that kind of relationship in South Carolina."

"I can't believe you have been able to hide it from your family. They ain't never wondered why you ain't have any girl-friends?"

"What you mean? I've had plenty girlfriends. I always keep a girl around if I'm going to be back home. I got a couple of baby mommas I got to keep happy."

"You got kids?"

"Yeah, I got three."

"Damn, you never told me that."

"Well bae, you never asked, and we just met. I am sure there's plenty more to find out about each other."

"This is interesting to me. So, tell me, how is it living this secret life? I mean, I've been out of the closet so long, I can't imagine what the closet feels like. Well, as if I was ever truly in a closet. I'm pretty sure everyone has known about me since I was a toddler walking in my momma's pair of heels."

"Never thought about it, but, I guess it can get lonely. When I'm out here on the road and no matter if I have good or bad times, I can't call home and talk about it with my family. And when I am back home and have good times with my family, I don't have anyone to share those moments with. It's a constant in and out of two different lives, but hey, it is what it is. I'm not complaining.

"Seems like a lot. What about your friends?"

"I ain't got any real friends. I got dudes I grew up with, but it's the same with them. Ain't trying to hurt anybody with my life choices. I just got to do what I got to do."

"But what if you're hurting yourself, bae?"

"I'm strong. Hell, I can deal. Life could be worse. I'm alive, making money, and taking care of my kids. No need to make drama if there doesn't have to be any. Y'all gays need to get off y'all high horses and enjoy the simple life. Let go of all these fabulous dreams and expectations."

"Well, wouldn't it just be easier for you to just be with a woman?"

"Wouldn't it just be easier for you to just be a man, like you were born?"

"Damn, I'm sorry. I didn't mean anything by the question, no need to be an ass, Mike."

"I'm sorry babe. It's just a sensitive subject for me, but honestly, I think my older brother knows about me."

"Why do you think that?"

"Brothers just know. It's some kind of weird bond we share. He has given me that look before like he knows, and I just stay quiet. I've learned silence is best."

"Well, baby, you ain't got to be silent with me. You can let it out, and be yourself. You can be free with me."

"That's good to know."

"This is our drop-off. Can you go outside and unlatch the trailer so we can go find something to eat?" I ask as we pull up to the warehouse where we were dropping the load off.

"No problem, baby, I got you," he says as he jumps out of the truck to take the trailer off.

As he began getting the trailer off, another truck driver walks up to him, and they began having a very long conversation. The other truck driver was a very old, fat, white man who looked like he could have been an extra on the first season of Roseanne. They both kept looking at me in the truck, and going back to what seemed like a deep conversation before the trucker left, and he reentered the truck.

"Thank you, baby," I say as he jumps back into the truck.

"No problem. Let me ask you something."

"Wassup, baby?"

"How much would you charge to let that white man fuck you?"

"Huh? What are you talking about? Why would I let him fuck me?"

"He walked up to me asking if I knew any dudes, or trannys, looking to make some big money. He offered $1500 for a night with nothing off limits."

"Boy, shut up! You're high as fuck!"

"So what if I am high? You high too. I told him you would let him fuck you with your wig on, and fake titties."

"Are you serious? Why would you tell him that? I am not a prostitute."

"Nigga, you need to get this money. Don't be stupid. If he offering you good money to fuck, then do it."

"You do it then, nigga. You got me fucked up!"

"Naw, bitch, you got me fucked up! I ain't gay! I'm not letting no nigga fuck me. You the one with wigs and shit. Let him fuck you like a bitch!"

"Fuck you! I'm ready to go, you trippin'! You look gay to me ,motherfucker!"

"Who the fuck are you talking to?" he says as he punches my head into the window.

"Damn, why would your punk ass hit me? I'm bleeding," I said when I realized I was bleeding from my head because of the impact of the window, and from my nose when he punched me.

"Because I can, fag," he said as he jumped on top of me and started choking me.

I immediately began to fight back. We turned that truck into a reenactment of Ike and Tina Turner from *What's Love Got to do With It*. I jumped out of the truck and began screaming for help. What the hell have I gotten myself into?

Eman

Five months, three days, and twelve hours, is how long Trayvon and I have been in a relationship. I must say it's been the best few months of my life. The boy is just a really good dude. We have definitely had a few bumps in the road, though. I had to cuss his ass out a couple of times about the messages he sends to other guys on yahoo messenger and black planet. He has also caught me texting a few old clients of mine trying to see if they can send me some money. I've only survived without a job because I got money from my family, and loans from guys I promised I would fuck later.

After my mom died, I decided it was time for me to get closer to my family, and get on some sort of positive life path. I really owed that to Trayvon. He is like my inspiration to do better. So far, we all have a plan to move to Atlanta in August. Even Robert is acting like he's going with us, but he stays in the hospital, so I'm not really sure if he will make it that long. I'm trying not to be pessimistic about his condition, but I've watched someone die, and it's no pretty picture.

I've actually decided to apply for FASFA, and hopefully I can enroll in a community college when I get down there. Jay Jay and I have been online looking up apartments to move to when we get there. Trayvon will be living on campus. He got a full ride to Morehouse College, and he decided to go there so we could still be together.

I am so excited about having my first grown up relationship. I never thought it would happen this soon.

"Why are you guys sitting so close together," asks GeGe (Trayvon's great-grandmother).

"OMG, GeGe! We are not sitting that close. Anyway, is it a crime to sit close to my boyfriend?"

"Listen here, you don't have to be freaky," she replies.

"What did I say that was freaky? I just said he was my boyfriend."

"That's freaky to me. I didn't even know you was even like that, Eman," she states.

"Like what, GEGE?"

"Fruity, gay, you know."

"Yes, ma'am, I am. I've been out for a minute now."

"Did your momma know?"

"Yeah, she did, and she was fine with it."

"I'm fine with it, too. Just don't be in here talking freaky, and holding hands, and stuff. Y'all do that at your house."

"Stop it, GeGe. No one is being freaky," Trayvon laughs.

"You lucky you smart, boy. I'm so proud of your scholarship. I told all the ladies at the senior building about your full scholarship," says GeGe.

"Thank you, GeGe. When is the church van getting here to pick us up?" Trayvon asks.

"You know Mr. Black will be here any minute. I'm about to go to the lobby and wait on him to pull up with the van. I'll push the buzzer to let you know that he's outside," GeGe says as she walks out of the apartment.

"Everything ok, Eman?" Tray asks.

"Yeah, I'm good. I'm just a little nervous about going to your church. I don't know how all of this works."

"Well, I don't either. All the kids in the youth group will be trying to figure out who you are, they're so nosey."

"What do I say if they ask who I am?"

"Just say you're a close friend of the family. Half of the men in that church is gay, so don't be scared. You will see queens walking around everywhere."

"I can only imagine, especially if you go there."

"Whatever, lady bug. Let's go wait in the lobby with GeGe. She starts tripping if I take too long getting to the van, and I don't want to give her a reason to get on my nerves," Trayvon adds as he grabs my hand and ushers me out of his great-grandmother's apartment.

Initially, it felt really weird entering the church. I hadn't been inside of a church building since my mother's funeral, and before then, I couldn't tell you the last time I attended a Sunday service. My mom went to church every so often, but she never mandated that I went, so I never felt the need to go. I believe in God, and consider myself spiritual, but I don't have time for the hypocrisy in the church.

The ride on the church van had been very interesting as Mr. Black and GeGe drove around picking up people throughout the city to bring to church. There were old people, young people, men, and women. All of them either didn't drive anymore, or just didn't have a car. The conversations and interactions were quite amusing, considering how new all of this was to me.

I've heard stories from Trayvon about how funny the church van could be, but hilarious is an understatement. Old folks and church folks throw a lot of shade to people, and they love gossiping about other people's business.

The church building was a fairly decent size church, definitely not a small congregation. It was gray in color, and it had a big cross on the front of the building with the words Detroit City Church of Christ written directly above it. Trayvon was immediately swarmed by little girls who wanted to give him a hug, and give him updates about their week at school and with family.

GeGe walked through the building like the queen bee of the congregation. She had been attending this church for over 40 years, so she knew everyone, and everyone knew her. They truly treated her like a queen. She immediately found her spot in the sanctuary to ensure no one took her spot, where she sat every Sunday for more than ten years.

I watched her put a peppermint in her mouth, take her mink off, and began talking to her neighbors in the pew as people filled up the sanctuary. Trayvon had me following him all around the church, introducing me to every single person that made eye contact. I caught a few guys looking at me longer than they should have, and others were giving me the side eye since it was apparent I was there with Trayvon. He made it very clear, and it made me nervous as hell.

I had never experienced being in a relationship publicly with a guy, and never in life would I have imagined being paraded around a church as another man's boyfriend. I was waiting for God to strike me down, but it never happened. Actually, nothing happened. Everyone made me feel quite comfortable, and I felt happiness on the inside. I wanted to grab Trayvon and kiss him for bringing me, and helping me feel like I did.

The choir began singing, and I immediately realized there was no band or instruments. Then, I realized they would be singing a cappella. I was very skeptical, at first, but then this lady got the mic for a solo, and she sent a dagger straight to my heart.

As they began singing in harmony, and making beats with their mouth, I began to feel Ma's presence. I felt like Ma was in the room with me amongst all the people in the church. I began to feel the spirit overcome my body, and I started clapping and stomping my feet to the song *Mansion, Robe, and Crown.*

Throughout the sermon, which was entitled, "Finding Your Purpose," I kept hearing Ma tell me to let go, and allow the words of the preacher to fill my soul. She cried in my ear, and told me she was waiting on me to come to her, and that she missed me. As the words of the preacher began touching me mentally, the Ma's words broke me down to the core while tears began streaming down my eyes.

Was this the feeling of God that I have been missing? Ma was with the Lord, and they were both speaking to me. The preacher began shouting and praising, and I could hear GeGe yelling back, "Preach preacher, preach" from across the church in a very monotoned way.

People were getting up and clapping. The room began to get hot, and I could feel the thumping under my feet from the explosion of the church experience with each pinnacle point of the preacher's sermon. The Lord had filled the place, and I was in a place I had never been before. I was feeling God.

"Are you okay Eman?" Trayvon asked as he watched the tears roll down my face.

"I think I wanna get baptized."

"Go ahead, Eman. Walk down the aisle, and be with the Lord."

After standing in front of the church, confessing my sins, and declaring to give myself to the Lord, I was taken to the back to undress. The deacons brought me back out at the top of the sanctuary in front of the whole congregation behind a river backdrop. Then the preacher submerged me under water, wrapped in white cloth, as my new life with God (and my mother) was birthed.

Robert

I always feel special when all of the fellas come visit me when I'm in the hospital. I love my mother and sister to death, but when the YaYa Sisterhood meets up, it's always a cackle, even if it's in the death hospital (also known as the Henry Ford Hospital). The doctor only gave me thirty days to live, and I haven't told anybody because I don't want everybody getting all sad before I actually die.

The chemotherapy isn't working, and the lymphoma is getting the best of me. I had to come back to the hospital because of the swelling. My leg has gotten so big, it looks like a damn watermelon. I'm not going to lie, I'm scared as fuck, but at this point, I have learned to start accepting leaving this world.

I pray my mother finds her a husband and becomes happy. I pray my sister raises my nephew and niece to be great people, and she finds another husband that won't put his hands on her. I pray Trayvon continues with his education, and becomes a lawyer and make a difference for queer people of color. I pray Eman finds a great path in life without his mom being here, and that great things go his way. Jay Jay, that damn Jay Jay. The person that has been my best friend forever. I pray the world is kind to this gentle and kind soul. Damn, I love Jay Jay.

"Do remember when you called Mrs. Chambers a bitch in English class, and she said she was gone fuck you up?" asks Jay Jay as he and the other guys stand around my hospital bed laughing and reminiscing.

"Okay, bitch! I do remember that. I told her if she wanted these hands, we could go outside. I got suspended for seven days for threats of violence. I hated that bitch," I responded.

"Why in the world would you call your teacher a bitch?" laughs Trayvon.

"Chile, I didn't give a fuck back then. I was the big fat class clown. I used to make everybody laugh."

"Yes, you did, bitch. I remember you and Crystal got into this big ass argument in Chinese class. You were calling her a dyke, and she was calling you a fag. Mrs. Chang was yelling for y'all to shut up, and y'all kept ignoring her," adds Jay Jay.

"No, bitches. Do you remember when you were vogueing at the Prodigy Ball for Virgin Vogue, and you busted a split on the runway. Bitch, the whole ball went crazy, and you won! You beat like ten people that night," says Eman.

"Yes, hunny. I was high as fuck, and I was processing the girls that night," I add, remembering very easily because it was the first time I ever walked and won.
I never really participated in the balls. I just liked watching them, and vogueing at home, and in my car.

"Girl, does your leg hurt?" asked Jay Jay.

"Bitch, they got me on some heavy drugs. I don't feel nothing. I know it looks bad, though," I add.

"You need to give me some of those pills, girl. You know I love a good ole prescription drug," says Jay Jay.

"Bitch, you love any drugs! You are starting to get that drug ring around your eyes. Slow down, girl. Mrs. Addict," I laugh off, even though Jay Jay is looking a little rough these days.
 I haven't spoken to him much since he got back on the road and started going through his transition.

"Your leg looks like Peaches' leg when Eman ran over her foot with your momma's car when they were fighting at the house party a few years ago," Trayvon says.

"I told that bitch, if she said anything else I was going to hit her with a car. So, I picked up Robert's keys off the porch, and tried to ram that hoe into the house. She almost got me arrested for attempted murder. I had to do five hundred hours of community service because of that hoe's smart ass mouth," Eman says, seemingly getting mad again just thinking about it.

"Eman, your ass totally blacked out. I tried to stop you from getting in that car, and you pushed me down to the ground. You lucky we all testified on your behalf, and they couldn't prove that you intentionally tried to run over her feet, or that you were drunk, since none of us originally called the police," I add.

"That dumb hoe walked around with a swollen foot, and kept partying until those drugs wore off the next day," Eman says.

"Jokes aside, how are you feeling, Robert?" asks Trayvon.

"I'm okay, for a guy who the doctors says only have thirty days to live," I respond.

"What? Don't say that, Robert," says Jay Jay.

"Girl, that's what he said. He doesn't know that I ain't going out like no punk bitch, though."

"That's the way you have to look at it, man. The doctors are not certain on anything. You were diagnosed a while back, and you're still here. They don't know what the hell they be talking about," says Eman.

"Well, I hope so, bitch! I want to at least live to see twenty six. Damn, the world doesn't want a bitch to be great," I jokingly say.

"Just know, we are here for you, bitch. Say the word, and I'll be up here. You ain't leaving us like Prue did in Charmed. The power of four will give you more," says Jay Jay.

"That's not how that works, bitch! It's the power of three," I respond.

"'Listen hoe, I'm being positive! I said four, so its four!" Jay Jay yells as all of us burst out in laughter together.
No matter the things we go through, there are no bonds so strong as those which are formed by suffering together.

Trayvon

It's here; graduation. This is the end of an era for me. I actually fucking did it, even though I doubted I would make it to this point. I always had dreams about how this day would feel, but I kept thinking about a statement my great aunt said when I saw her the other day. She told me I grew up to look just like my father. For others, I believe that would have been a lovely thing to hear, maybe even a proud moment to know you grew into a man that replicates their father. That's not necessarily the case for me because my father is a man that I have never seen, or met in my life.

I've seen pictures from time to time over the years, but I never actually met him. I wonder how I survived seventeen years on this earth never knowing him, or anybody on the paternal side of my family. Do I look like any of them? Do I have cousins that I have slept with and didn't know? Does my grandmother ever ask about me? Does she know I exist? Where does a fatherless boy look for answers to what's next in his life?

I could cry about not having a father, but what good does that do? That will not make me know him any better. I could cry about how he left me to be raised by a stepfather, and how my stepfather used my face as punching bag in between his bottles of thunderbird and his meetings with crack pipe. Since I wasn't his biological son, he treated me differently from my sisters, and my feminine ways didn't help with how he felt about me.

He often told my mom that he was going to beat the fag out of me. He said that until I grew old enough to know that I had to start hitting him back. I will never forget the day I took his insulin, filled a needle with it, and jammed into his heart while he slept. I tried to kill him, but unfortunately, it didn't work. That just began the life or death matches I would have to endure much of my entire pre-teen years.

This is why I moved in with my great grandmother, GeGe. She took me in when no one else would. Everyone says I was a

bad child because of my smart-ass mouth. My mom didn't have
the time, or the skills, to raise me. And without a father, I was on
the brink of being raised by society.

GeGe gave me stability and security. She has always been
my biggest cheerleader, and she always expected me to accomplish big things. I never wanted to let her down. We have lived in
her small apartment in the senior community for the last four
years, and I have my best moments in life laid across the foot of
her bed, watching the news and Jeopardy while we talked about
life.

For her to be an older woman, she was very accepting of
my lifestyle, and she always gives me great advice based on her
on own life experiences. After having eight brother and sisters,
two husbands, seven kids, and five step-children, she definitely
has lived a life. A man couldn't be happier than to look at the joy
in her and my mother's eyes on graduation day knowing they are
proud of me, and my future. Having their love puts bandages over
the hole of not having a father. Maybe one the bandages will un-
ravel, but today, I'm letting those feelings of abandonment go, and
enjoy the present.

"Who picked this place?" asks GeGe.

"I did. I've wanted to come to this Chinese buffet. I asked
Trayvon what he wanted to eat, and he said Chinese," my mother
said.

"No, I wasn't complaining. It's very clean, and the food is
good. I'm glad I brought my Ziploc bags so I can sneak some food
for later," says GeGe.

"GeGe, you are always taking food home. Have you ever
just had a meal without any leftovers?" I asked.

"What are you talking about, boy? You stay in the refriger-
ator eating all of my leftovers"

"I know I do. You bring home some good food."

"So, what's y'all plans down in Atlanta, Eman and Jay Jay?"
my mom asks.

"Well, I just enrolled into Atlanta Community College to study finance," says Eman.

"And I'm going to Atlanta School of Design next year. I didn't get my application in on time for next semester. I'm going to keep driving trucks for now, so I can have money to pay rent for our apartment," Jay Jay responds.

"Well, y'all be careful down there. I'm glad y'all going down together to help each other out. I'm so nervous for Trayvon to move so far away. I don't know why y'all want to move to the south with those country folks," laughs my mother.

"It's not that country down there, Ma," I respond.

"I saw on the news they have an HIV epidemic down there," my mom says.

"Yeah, I saw that, too. That is so scary," Eman responds.

"You and Trayvon better be using a condom. That HIV shit ain't no joke you hear me?"

"We do use condoms, thank you very much. You can catch HIV anywhere, there are just more black gays in Atlanta, and the stats reflects the reality across the country," I defensively respond.

"Can you change the subject? We are in public, and anyways, my sister is down there with her family. Make sure you visit her," interrupts GeGe.

"I will, GeGe, don't worry."

"And make sure y'all find a church home down there, preferably a Church of Christ. Eman, you just got baptized, you can't afford to fall backwards," she adds.

"I won't, GeGe. I don't think Trayvon will allow that to happen," says Eman as he gives me a smile that melts my heart.

I used to always talked about how I couldn't wait until I was grown so I could do what I wanted to do. Even though I pretty much did what I wanted to do during my high school years, nothing could have prepared me for the awesome feeling of freedom. It was also frightening to think I now had to make decisions for myself, and make sure I was doing the right things.

I don't have GeGe, or my momma trying to say what I could or couldn't do. All I have now, is Tray. I just hope the world is kind to me, as I will continue to be kind to it. If I put forth good energy, good energy should come back to me. I've always considered myself to be blessed in my life because when I thought it couldn't get any better, it did, and for that I will always be thankful.

Eman decided to take me to my favorite place on earth; Cedar Point Amusement Park in Ohio. He knows I love amusement parks and getting on rides, even though he doesn't like them so much. He will get on a ride with me just to make me happy, but he is a scary cat. He swears he's so gangsta, but he can't even get on a merry go round without crying. I have to remind him all the time to suck it up, and be a man. He gets so mad when I do that.

Last year, we came here on Father's Day for Gay Day, and we had been drinking in the car the whole drive down there. By the time we finished the second ride, he was bent over, throwing up in a corner. He had to sleep in the car for hours so he wouldn't ruin everybody's day and make us have to drive back home. He just couldn't hang.

He brought me here today for a late graduation gift and birthday outing with his lesbian cousin, and her girlfriend. It's a couple's trip, and we have on "his and his" shirts, and they have on "hers and hers" shirts. We are really turning this park out today, but who cares?

I am eighteen now, and Eman is almost twenty. We don't have any reasons to be apologetic about who we are. We gay as fuck! His cousin is really out there, though. She is harder than Eman and I combined, and she is very aggressive. She has already tried to fight two dudes for looking at her girl. I'm so glad they decided to get on a few rides without us because they were making my nerves bad with all their drama.

"Why are you looking like that?"

"Really, you are really going to ask me that?"

"What?"

"You know what, Eman. Your cousin is crazy as fuck."

"Ha, what are you talking about, Tray?"

"She just told that dude she was going back to her car to get her gun out the trunk so she could cap his ass."

"Okay, she does have her gun in the car. She doesn't go anywhere without it."

"It ain't that serious."

"What you mean, it ain't that serious? He smacked her girl on the ass. I would fuck a nigga up if they would ever touch you."

"True, but it doesn't help that her girlfriend is walking around with her ass hanging out. I can literally see traces of her pussy hair. There are kids out here."

"Boy, I know you gone let her dress like she wants to. Hell, it's hot out here."

"She can still at least put her shirt back on. She is too big to be walking around here like that. That's only a sports bra, nasty ass."

"Baby, calm down! They are gone, and please don't get mad at me for what my cousin's girlfriend is wearing, Hell I don't know her."

"I ain't mad. They just got me all anxious with all this drama. I get nervous with all that fighting with straight people. Y'all used to all that, but I don't hang out with straight people. You remember the last time we fought a bunch of straight dudes? I got knocked out, and you had a busted nose."

"Yeah, I remember. I feel you, but all that is not important. Are you enjoying yourself? Are you enjoying your birthday?"

"Yeah I am. Thank you for bringing me down here to get away for the day."

"Boy, stop it! This ain't nothing, baby. We are turning up tonight. My baby is grown now. We gone make tonight a night to remember, and cap it off with some bomb ass sex."

"Sounds like a good night to me."

"Yeah, there will be plenty of sounds."

"You so nasty!"

"Yeah, real nasty."

Eman

Another year, another pride. It's hard to say it doesn't get old, but I guess it could be fun if you really get into it. It can be the best weekend of the year, if it all goes right. They say you get out of it what you put into it. I just don't get hyped to be around the fags, I just don't. I love my gay family and the YaYa Sisterhood, but I could give zero fucks about the rest.

These girls will lie, steal, and kill over the dumbest shit, and I'm just at a different place in life. Last year, that shit that went down at pride was crazy! Beating that boy up was too much, and that's not including all the stupid shit that happened before and after. They need to start locking these girls up. I mean, I'm always down for a good fight but when you got bullets flying everywhere, and homes getting burglarized, it's time to get these girls in orange jumpsuits. Hell, they're acting like they have nothing to live for, so let's get rid of them. If my gay daddy is getting locked up, I want the other low-life girls in there, too.

My gay daddy, is also my house daddy. He is the one who brought me into the ballroom scene when I was 15. My house is known as the realness house in Detroit. We got all the realness categories on lock, and we win all the realness categories at most balls. I have won "Pretty Boy Realness of the Year" for two years in row because I always win. I have never lost here. I have lost at balls in Chicago and New York, but even those battles were close.

My gay daddy single handily put Detroit on the ballroom map for realness. It doesn't help that our city is the murder capital, and has a dangerous reputation across the country. He is legendary in his category of Thug Realness, and also wins in a lot of label categories such as Foot, Eye, Belt, and Best Dressed Spectator. He is not the overall father of the House of Dollars for nothing.

He is the definition of a hustler or baller. He wears furs and diamonds, and keeps a safe full of money in his house. He doesn't leave his house without a few thousand dollars. Most of the leadership of the house all drive Cadillac Escalades, and have several homes on Jefferson Avenue, right off the Detroit River.

Last year for Christmas, he bought all the pretty boys mink coats, and we walked a ball in Chicago as realness, as a house, and we won the grand prize money of one thousand dollars. Money is never an option in our house, but I have never been a fool. I knew there were illegal activities, and I always stayed away from them. I didn't allow my father to get me cars because I was too scared to drive around in them, or pay rent with dirty money.

My father did his part of keeping me out of the loop, and not letting me know where the money was coming from. He also ignored all of my questions when I was trying to be nosey. I've been told from friends that they were into check fraud, but I've also heard bank robbery. Nothing has been confirmed to me, though.

Our house members have been getting arrested left and right, and when I found out my father was one, I actually cried. On the news, they said they had embezzled over one million dollars, and he was sentenced to seven years in federal prison with only a week to turn himself in. I just can't believe this shit! This man has truly been a father to me; the father I never had. He taught me to be hard, he taught me how to fight, and he taught me how to hustle; now he is going to prison.

Our house is hosting this year's Detroit Awards Ball that happens every pride. It's going to be like a farewell ball, or an "end to an era," but an awards ceremony, as well. He pitched a lot of different ideas to the ballroom committee, and we were selected to host the ball in a very competitive process. This ball will also be my farewell to the Detroit ballroom scene, and my house because after I move to Atlanta, I'll probably join another house.

Our house doesn't have a presence in the south and, without a strong family supporting you, it can be hard to win balls in a different city. Hell, I might just leave the ballroom scene altogether, and just support Tray when he walks. I love to see my baby eat it up on the runway.

We have been promoting this ball heavily, and I have been a part of the planning from the beginning. I was involved in the flyer design, creating and writing the categories, decorating the tables, and picking the judges and prize money. I actually have been in charge of the whole ball, and actually felt good I was trusted with the task and have been able to actually complete it.

We all decided to have the ball at the Post. One reason is because my father manages the hall for club promotions, so the cost to rent is low. Secondly, almost every ball in the city is here. The girls are familiar with the venue. The DJ booth is set up, the tables are decorated, and the bar is fully stocked, so all I have to do is setup the trophies, and start getting dresses. All that can wait though, I need a cocktail.

"How you expect us to make money if you drinking the liquor at the bar?" yells my gay father as he is walking into the Post, and catching me behind the bar.

"Stop it nigga, this is my first drink."

"Where is ya personal bottle, nigga? You know better than to drink the liquor for the bar. What if we run out, huh? We ain't making no money. I got a bottle of Hennessy in the trunk of the car."

"I don't drink no damn Hennessy."

"You are tonight! And get ya ass from behind that bar unless you want to be the bartender all night."

"Nah, I'm good on that, Pops."

"I thought so. When you gone set up the trophies?"

"I got it. Damn, chill pops. Why you acting all excited and shit?"

"Nigga, my anxiety is on 100. I am going crazy, shit! My ass is going to federal prison in two days."

"I don't want to talk about it. I ain't trying to get my feelings right now!"

"Not talking about it doesn't change shit. It's life. I got caught trusting some pussy ass snitches!"

"You scared?"

"Nigga, nah. I have been to prison before. I did five years back when I was nineteen. The most I'm going to do is three years, I ain't got no reason to be scared."

"I feel ya, Pops, but I'm gone miss you. Three years is a long time."

"You planned on leaving me anyway, running behind that cute little chocolate boy, Tray, to Atlanta."

"You can move to Atlanta, too."

"Boy, hell nah! I ain't moving down there with all those queens. I like to visit ATL during Labor Day weekend, but my black ass staying in Detroit. I love Detroit!"

"Why, though? This city is dead."

"Nigga, you crazy! This the city for the players and pimps. Nobody got flavor like Detroit. I've been all around this country, and nothing compares to the D."

"You can have the D. I'm ready to go!"

"Good. You still wrong, but ain't nothing wrong with you going on to live other places and meet new people. Just don't forget where you came from. I need you to create a chapter of our house down there in Atlanta. I think you ready to be house father down there."

"I don't know about that, Pops."

"What you mean, you don't know? Your ass been asking since last year to be given a chance to be a house father, and now you don't know. You a trip."

"I just been thinking that I want to do something different with my life."

"And you should. You graduated from high school, and hopefully you taking your ass to college, and doing something better. All that doesn't mean you have to leave ballroom. Bring that shit back to ballroom. Elevate this shit, and start making money! Nigga, you got a legacy to keep up. Ballroom raised you.

"You right! Do you think I can really do it? You gone be gone. I can't do this shit without you. Who would I turn to when I need help?"

"Yourself, nigga! You turn to your damn self! Don't depend on nobody but yourself. Get a team with new house members. Your little boyfriend Tray always winning runway, so get his ass to join the house. What's your other friend's name? The trans girl?"

"Jay Jay. Well, her name is Jazmine now."

"Yeah, her. That's a pretty bitch! I can see her slaying all the female figure categories. Son, I need you to keep this house alive while I'm gone. I taught you all you need to know. You understand?"

"Yeah, Pops, I do. I got you."

"Alright then, little nigga. Now, get your ass up and get those trophies where they need to be. I'm going to get the Hennessy out of the car, I need a drink. It's time to get this ball started.

Robert

Dear God, I told my mother I want them to make sure that somebody sings *Endow Me* by The Clark Sisters at my funeral, preferably the actual Clark Sisters, themselves. As she sat next me in the hospital bed, she said that she would do her best. I also told her I wanted Jay Jay to do a performance of *One Sweet Day* by Mariah Carey and Boys II Men, and she squeezed my hand tightly, and she told me she didn't know about that one. I didn't have the strength to fight with her. She betta let Jay Jay sing, though.

I love when she rubs my head when we talk. I can barely move, but when her fingers brushes across my head, I feel heaven. Why haven't I known all this time that my momma's touch was so heavenly? I could have used her touch during all the hard times I went through in my life. Who would have known my momma was magical? And why didn't you tell me, God?

Maybe she was saving her magic for my sister and my nephew to protect them, and maybe she didn't have enough magic for all of us. Life seems to always have a way to hide our treasures, and somehow, someway, we have to find them. I'm glad, that on this day, and at this time, I got to feel the magic of my momma. It couldn't have come at a better time, so thank you momma.

Dear God. Tell Eman to stop laughing so hard. He making me laugh too and it hurts to laugh, but this feeling is so good. It feels good to laugh with Eman and watch this beautiful man peel back all his layers and simply bloom. This is beautiful to be a part of and he is beautiful. What was on your mind when you molding him in your image? His hair is beautifully laid on his head, teeth is glowing as he speak with beautiful Spanish accent. His presence is mesmerizing and strong, a presence of a king destined to lead his people. Looking at him makes me feel Heaven and brings me joy. I wonder if its guys in Heaven that looks like him. He is wearing the cologne I got him for Christmas and his smell is perfect, and I close my eyes as we speak, I can smell him and its beautiful.

I feel weak but knowing that he is right beside me in this hospital bed, I have to take another glance at his beauty. I love Eman with your pretty ass.

Dear God, you outdid yourself with Trayvon. I wonder if there are other angels walking the earth among us like he does. His spirit is full of good vibes, and when he speaks, I feel better. His spirits feels up the room with the love and concern, and it literally lifts me up when I speak with him, but I have one request. Tell the boy to shut up. He is talking a million miles per minute, and my brain just can't keep up. It's cute though because he is giving me all the latest tea, and giving me all the updates about him and Eman. He also gives me all of the drama with Jay Jay, and that boy Mike.

Trayvon is my baby, and I'm proud of the man he is becoming. He is a man of substance, and a man of good character. If I'm dying like the real Prue from Charmed, I feel at peace knowing that Paige is here in the sisterhood to keep it going. I feel his spirit fill the room, and I no longer feel like we're sitting in this hospital bed. Instead, I feel like we are in the car riding through the city... talking.

We are talking about everything and nothing at the same time. He likes to debate, he likes to argue, but that's because he is smart. He is kind, he is caring, and as his spirit continues to fill the room with warmth and love, I feel a cold breeze. I am getting cold in my body, and I wrap myself in the covers. I indulged all of my energy to match his energy. Talk to me, Trayvon. I love when we talk. You say things so honestly, and you don't even realize how pure your heart is. Talk to me, Trayvon. I love when we talk. You say things so intelligently, and you don't even realize how great your mind is. I stay awake to hear you talk. I love when we talk. Thank you, Tray.

Dear God, can I just stay on earth a little while longer? I want to make more memories with my best friend, Jay Jay. It's him I worry about the most. He is the one who has always been there to share my thoughts with. He is the one I am always able to share where my heart belongs. He is the one that gave me strength when I thought I had no more to give. All the times I thought today would be the day that I would die, he was the one I looked to, to find the will to live.

He's the most fragile one, and he was beside me in this hospital bed. He smells of the day old staleness of liquor seeping through my nose. His eyes stares back at me with the pupils of ecstasy and gaze of fear. He is why I pray to live forever as a guardian angel. I pray I can continue to look over him, and guide him through the crucial period of his life that we always intended to share.

As I lay, I know I must leave my sister and be with you, but it is he that keeps me with one foot in heaven, and one foot here with him. He needs me, and I need him. With you, we're all we got. My sister is she, and she is I. So, I pray that as you take me away, and I breathe my last breath, that you promise that I am not saying good bye to my sister, but rather see you later. Let my sister live, and let her live well. My sister is he, and he is I.

I'll come to her in her dreams, so we will not part too far. I'll show up through her tears to help her dry her eyes. I feel you God, telling me time to go, but I'm scared. I will miss these people. These people I hurt so much, and at the same time, loved so much. These people are within me, and I am within them. We are she. We are he. We are us. I hear you God, saying it's time to go, but can I please have more time? My eyes are getting heavy. My body is getting cold. I don't even think I have thoughts anymore, but somehow I'm here. I'm present, but I have descended. I'm coming God.

Jay Jay

So it's real, and Jazmine is definitely starting to emerge. I thought long and hard about if this was truly the step I wanted to take. After several therapy sessions, long nights with my gay mother, and long nights with Robert at the hospital, I have decided to continue down the road of transitioning. I had started taking some hormones I was getting off the black market, but now that my insurance from the trucking company is effective, I've began taking the real stuff.

The people at the Ruth Ellis Center also have been helping me out at our vogue session nights with group therapy about transgender women of color. My insurance has already approved my hair removal, and now they have approved my hormone replacement therapy that I have to figure out how to stay on for the rest of my life. I'm not in a rush to get a Vaginoplasty at all. I'm not in a rush because for one, I don't have the coins to pay for it right now.

I recently filed a petition to change my name with the Circuit Court, and I am scheduled to appear before the judge right before we sign the lease to the new apartment in ATL. Even though I am moving forward with this, I am scared as fuck. I've always boasted about being a lady and being cunt, but now I have to put my money where my mouth is. I'm not going to be one of these boys out here claiming to be transgendered, I'm going to be a lady, and carry myself as such.

Jazmine is here, and she will transcend into this world with style and grace. Outside of my best friend being laid up in the hospital clinging on to dear life, I am in a very good space. The guy I was driving trucks with, Mike, and I are doing better. He still gets crazy every now and then, and wants to fight, but I just play the role and let him get it out. Besides the few hits to the head every now and then, it's actually a really good relationship. Robert thinks I'm crazy for staying in the situation, but he doesn't understand what girls like me go through.

I've never had a boyfriend because guys didn't like boys like me. Most guys in Detroit like gay guys who act straight; homo thugs. This is the first time I had a man who loved me for me, and I'm not letting that go because he has a bad temper. I'm twenty-four years old, and I need to experience what a relationship feels like. Hell, if Trayvon and Eman can be in a relationship, I can be in a relationship with Mike's crazy ass. Plus, we're making a lot of money.

Outside of the checks we are getting from the trucking company, I've been servicing guys on the side from time to time. I can easily make over five hundred dollars a night. I don't know what the hell Eman was doing all this time, but he was broke when he was prostituting compared to the coins I'm making. Mike thinks he's my pimp, but I do all the work. He is just more like my body guard in case some crazy shit go down with these dudes.

They be asking me to do a lot of freaky shit. One guy asked for me to shit on him, and I did it. Hell, he paid me $1000. You would be amazed at the things these white men like to do in the backwoods of rural Kansas. When I'm on the road with Mike, I feel free, living my new life. Sometimes, it's hard to come home to look at where I'm coming from.

This city is depressing. Watching Robert die is heartbreaking, so I am just ready to move. I promised Eman I would come home and pack my shit, so we can go. I'm so ready to go.

"Bitch, I didn't even know your ass was here. You stay on that road," says Eman as he walked into the living room.

"Yeah, I got in about an hour ago. I heard you and Trayvon fucking when I walked in there door. Y'all need to close the door when y'all gone have sex. I brought Michael with me this time, and his ass was being all nosey, trying to watch.

"Who the fuck is Michael?"

"The one I been on the road with. The one I'm dating."

"Oh, the man that's been giving you black eyes and shit!"

"Shut up, bitch! He can hear you!"

"Good. Robert told me about what he's been doing to you on the road."

"What the fuck? Why would he tell you anything? That is not any of your business."

"Chill out, man. I am not tripping, that's your business. If you want a man hitting on you, and selling ya ass like a piece of meat, then by all means, be with him. I'm not judging you. Just be careful, bitch."

"I guess. Back to you and Trayvon fucking with the door open."

"Girl, you must like what you heard, or saw. I've been told I have a good stroke game," says Trayvon coming out the room, interrupting our conversation.

"Girl, please. I ran in the bathroom to throw up from the sounds Eman was making, and from the thought of you fucking anybody, little lady."

"Bitch, please! You wish, Miss Jazmine," says Trayvon in his most effeminate voice.

"What brings you here with the common folk? I haven't see you in weeks," asks Eman.

"Damn, do I need a reason to come home? I brought Michael here with me so he could help me pack. Clearly, you two late queens haven't started packing yet. Everything still looks the same," I add.

"I told Eman to start packing, and I'll help. He is being so lazy, though"

"Don't lie, Travyon. You haven't said shit! We've been too busy getting ready for this ball in Chicago this weekend. Since you're here, bitch, we should all go together," Emans says.

"I got to ask Michael. I don't know if he's into that kind of stuff."

"Where is he? Why is he locked up in the room?"

"Because my trade knows not to be mingling with my friends like that. He don't know y'all," I jokingly respond.

"Girl, he can stay in there all day if he wants. I don't care to see Ike Turner anyway," says Eman.

"Well, bitch, they do say my legs look Tina Turner. Maybe I should get them insured. I'm looking like a tall glass of water," I add.

"Bitch, please! With all of those bumps and blemishes, looks more like a sea salt ocean with waves and pollution," Trayvon jokingly adds.

"Baby, your legs look good to me," says Michael as he walks into the living room.

"Thanks, baby. I know they are just hating, boo," I respond nervously.

"Oh, hey. You must be Michael, nice to meet you," Trayvon says.

"Nice to you meet you, too," Michael responds.

"And this is Eman, baby. He is my roommate," I add, noticing the tension between Michael and Eman.

"That's wassup," Michael whispers.

"Cool, cool," whispers Eman as he walked away, showing no interest in shaking Michael's hand.

"Guess what I was thinking we should do for our last night here in the apartment?"

"What is it, girl?"

"We should do a pageant," he responds.

"Really, baby? A pageant? We haven't done one of those in so long,"says Eman.

"I know. I think it would be fun if we invite some people over to help pack, and we could drink, smoke, and have a pageant in between. Us three can compete, and Michael, and whoever shows up, can vote on the winner," explains Trayvon as he approaches Eman to get him to agree.

"Who says I want to dress up and sing in front of this dude? I don't even know him," says Eman aggressively.

"Yo, bruh, I don't give two fucks about what you want to do man."

"I think you need to watch your tone, homeboy. You really don't want to know me bruh," says Michael walking towards Eman and Trayvon.

"Come on guys, stop it. Let's just have a good time, and have fun. No need for all this," I said, grabbing Michael by the arm to calm down.

"Calm down, man. You are coming off a little strong there. I was just joking. I'm good. You good?" asked Eman as he began to extend out his hand.

"I'm good, man. I just didn't know if we was good or not," Michael adds.

"We good, man," says Eman as they shake hands, and seemingly let their guards down.

We gave each other thirty minutes to get our wardrobe and music together for our ghetto house pageant. This was something that we did once a year to have fun, and just pay tribute to all the queens before us. It was something that Robert and I really loved doing because it reminded us of the pageants we used to go to in the early 90's.

We would sneak out of the house, and Robert would drive us to some hole-in-the-wall to see the ladies lip-sync for their lives. I eventually moved more into the ballroom scene, but Robert loved the pageant scene. He even served on the board for Mr. and Ms. Detroit Conferential. The main rule for our pageant was that you had to be creative. Anything pre-made, or put together, didn't get higher scores than something you cut up and put together yourself.

Sheets and pillow cases were always the first causalities, and we usually raided one of our momma's closets to get heels and jewelry. Since we were in our own apartment, I allowed the girls to use some of my wigs and accessories. I wasn't worried because I knew Trayvon and Eman wasn't a match for me. Hell, I'm a real woman now. Only Robert would even be competition. We had three rounds, and the judges voted me the winner in all three rounds. Trayvon got too drunk to even pay attention, and Eman spent more time trying to freak than to actually win. I was sipping on my winner's cocktail when my phone kept ringing over and over.

"Who keeps calling you?"

"I don't know, baby. Let me go see. It could be my mom," I respond wondering who would keep calling me after not getting any response.

"Hello!"

I stood there, frozen as ice, as my mom began to tell me Robert passed away a few hours ago. The tears began falling from my face, as I tried to come to grips that my best friend was gone.

Trayvon

Roberts's death is so unreal to me. I'm so full of emotions, that my mind is racing a million miles a minute. Even though he and I have had a rocky few months, and we might not have been as close as we were previous years, I have to acknowledge his importance in my life. If it wasn't for him, I probably wouldn't been able to navigate through this gay life. He was truly a great friend, and would have given his life to me if I had asked for it.

He was the one who took me to my first club. He took me to my first ball. Hell, he even gave me my first drink, and supplied most of the drugs I have ever taken. He was always available to talk when I was having boy issues and shit. His heart was always in a good place when it came to me, but his own demons and insecurities are what made it hard to be his friend sometimes. He just couldn't shake it. He lived to be accepted by others, and what people thought about him really mattered.

He was always looking for love in the wrong places because he didn't possess the power to love himself. He spent most of his gay life seemingly in a tug a war between good and evil, and this gay life chewed him up and spit him out. When I met him, he was successful, making decent money, and had several cars. By the time he got sick, he was jobless and stuntin' in his momma's vehicles, and he stayed at home in his childhood room.

He was always the funny one, and he loved to make people laugh, but what I've come to learn is that there is always hurt behind every joke. He was hurting, and most of us thought it was because of his weight issues. Maybe the weight issues opened up more doors that allowed pain to overtake him.

He had a lot of friends, and he knew most of the gays in Detroit, but in my heart, I feel like he died alone. When you don't give yourself to people honestly, those bonds that you create with them, are easily broken. I feel guilty about it because I knew I could have been there for him. I could have brought food to the hospital, or maybe spent more time talking to him, but it was just all too much for me. Just too stressful, and I had to focus on school, and not all the grown-up problems like sickness, and death.

I wondered if his illness helped recover some of the toxic relationships he had. He knew he was dying, and I feel like he wanted to make up for all the bad shit that had happened. The last few times we were all around each other was some of the best moments we had. His spirit seemed to be in a better place, and he was in a good place with all of us. He was kinder, he was gentler, he was a better person, and I was learning to love him all over again. We were all in a good place, and now he's gone. Just thinking about him makes me miss hearing his loud laugh. Damn! I am going to miss my friend.

Eman and I have been in a very weird place lately. I just think he doesn't know how to react to Roberts's death. He knows Jay Jay and I knew they had a rocky relationship, but I know he loved him. Maybe the same guilt I felt, he feels times ten worse. Not to mention, he lost his mother not too long ago. I am not being really accepting of him trying to make me feel better because he is walking around like he feels nothing. Just too many emotions right now, and my God, this is hard!

I can't find the words to judge him because I don't know how it feels not to have a mother, and lose a friend in the same year. I am just doing my best in making sure he is okay.

"What did the leasing lady say?" I ask as Eman walked back into the apartment.

"She said it was fine for us to stay one more month. We just have to pay the month-to-month fee which is an additional two hundred dollars, plus the monthly rent," says Eman.

"A month! Why would we need a whole month? I have to move into my dorm room in a few weeks!"

"I know Tray, but that's the only way. You can't do an extension for a few weeks. It has to be a full month."

"How will you and Jay Jay be able to afford to pay an extra month here, when you are already paying the down payment for the new place in Atlanta?"

"He says he is making all this money, always bragging about his side hustles. I am sure he'll be able to come up with something. I've paid for everything by myself for months, while he was here. It's his turn to step up, and pay more. Besides, his best friend dying, changed our plans."

"Don't say that. Why would you say that? He was all of our friends. You are obligated to stay, and go to the funeral just like the rest of us."

"I ain't got to do shit!"

"Really! Don't forget he came to your mother's funeral, and supported you. Stop acting like that."

"I know, Tray. My bad! I didn't mean to say it like that. There's just a lot going on, and I'm starting to get stressed out."

"Yeah, too much going on, and where has Jay Jay been? I haven't seen him in a couple of days."

"He left, saying he was going over to Robert's mom's house to see what all she needed help with. He texted me yesterday and said he was going back to the road with Michael and has not re-sponded to any of my text messages since then."

"I know he is really going through it, and I hope Michael is doing him right. He don't need added drama with his damn pimp."

"Michael ain't that bad. And he ain't his pimp, remember?"

"Are you okay?"

"I'm cool, for the most part. I'm alive. What more can I ask for?"

"I'm just making sure. I know you just lost your mom, and all of this with the move..."

"I'm fine. Everything is going to go as planned. We are go-ing to handle this business with our boy, Robert, load these cars up, and hit the road. We gone get your ass to school on time, and start our new lives. If anything, since the loss of Mom, I've become more fearless. Ain't nothing going to break me."

The clouds are so gray today. It seems like every time there is a funeral, it rains outside. It's raining like cats and dogs. I really don't like funerals, but there is no way I wasn't coming to Robert's funeral. He was our sister.

Eman and I got ready in silence today. I ironed his clothes and laid them out for him before he woke up. He was tossing and turning all night, and he was sweating all over the place. These nightmares, as he calls them, have been happening more frequently lately. It scares me, but I can't help him. I have tried to talk to him about it, but it seems to only push him further away. So, I just wait until he comes around to talk.

We talk all night about how his mom comes to him and gives him encouraging words and guidance, and by the end of each dream, his mom gets murdered. He says he tries to wake up before she is murdered, but he never knows when it's going to happen because she dies differently in each nightmare.

The last nightmare he had, he told me that I poisoned his mom at dinner, and her face fell into a bowl of clam chowder. I didn't know if I should laugh, or be concerned about the nightmares. I just listened, instead. After ironing his clothes, I took a long hot shower, and cried thinking about Robert. I thought about heaven and hell, and wondered where he went. My heart says he went to heaven. I think about all the good and the bad, but again, my hearts says he went to heaven. I think about how I was raped in the back seat of his car, but my heart still says he went to heaven.

Jay Jay

Robert and I spent hours talking about what would happen during the days after he died. Most of the time, he would be cracking jokes about how his momma and grandmother would react. Or how Eman would be talking shit, but would be trying to sing a song at the funeral. That crazy motherfucker always knew how to make me laugh, even when joking about his own death.

He knew was dying so I can't say I was shocked when I got the call from my mom, especially after the last time I saw him. He was barely recognizable from all the swelling. His face was big and round like the old Robert, but this time, it was a little distorted. He even joked about how he didn't lose all this weight just to get fat again. Man, he was so damn crazy!

One thing we never discussed was how I was going to feel after he died. Who would have thought I would be planning my best friend's funeral in my early twenties? This is not unusual for young black gay males; it really is just our reality. Our lives seem very disposable, since we're dropping like flies in the summer time. Robert wasn't always the safest man when it came to sex. He even told me if he had to leave this world, it better be from some bomb ass raw dick. I can't really blame him because everybody likes raw sex, not just gays, everybody.

I charge more for my services if my client requests raw sex. The mentality for most gays is that we will end up with HIV anyway, so why stress about it? Personally, I haven't been tested in years because I don't wanna know, and once I'm ready to cross that bridge, I will. I very rarely get asked what my status is, and if they ask me, I tell them I'm negative. Hell, the last time I checked, it was negative. There was no need in telling them I got tested five years ago. And besides, it's none of their fucking business!

Ever since Robert's passing, I have distanced myself from people. I don't think I have the mental space to be peacemaker, or be fake with all these so-called friends. Half of the people that have been calling me, were not there for him while he was in and out of the hospital.

Every time I was able to go back to Detroit, I would help his mom with anything she needed. All these girls are just calling to get some tea. They asking, "Girl what happened?" or "How did he die?" If any of those bitches would have visited him, they would have known already.

I definitely have been keeping my distance from Trayon and Eman because, again, I feel they could have done more. I understand that they had their issues with him, but damn, we were friends; The YaYa Sisterhood. Robert did some fucked up things, but he did some good shit, too. When he needed us the most, all they could do was visit every so often because they were so busy. I am not saying Robert didn't appreciate when they visited, but I guess I feel some kind of way about it. I truly believe if they weren't in a relationship, things would have played out a lot of differently.

Trayvon would have forgiven Robert months ago, and they would have gone back to the way they were back in the day. He was influenced by Eman, and they had to put up a united front. Like anybody cares how they felt as a couple, anyway. I do have to understand they are young. They are not even legal enough to drink. They appear to be a lot older than they are, but it just that; an appearance. I just want to bury my best friend, and get back on road for a minute. I am in no mood to move to Atlanta right now.

"Did you finalize the menu yet, Mrs. Diane?" I ask Robert's mom while she sat on the porch, smoking a cigarette in her suburban neighborhood a few miles up the road from my mom house.

"No I haven't, yet. Hey, I need to talk to you real quick."

"Ok, what's up?"

"Well, I know I said you could speak at the funeral, but are you gonna be dressed like that?"

"Dressed like what?"

"Dressed up like a girl. I mean, this is my baby's funeral, and I just don't want all the negative drama with the family saying I let a drag queen speak at my son's funeral."

"Well, your son was my best friend, and he accepted me as I am. So, yes, I planned on speaking like this. Mrs. Diane, I am transwoman. I am not a drag queen."

"Same difference, and the rest of the family didn't know that side of Robert. They didn't know about y'all, and all of this gay stuff. Don't get me wrong, I love ya. Believe me, I do, I'm just tired, and I don't need the added drama. His family cared about him, too."

"Are you saying you don't want me to speak at the funeral?"

"I'm saying if you come as a boy, then fine you can speak, but if you plan on being made all up, I would prefer that you didn't. Why is this a big deal? You telling me you can't act like a man long enough for this funeral. I'm pretty sure your mom misses her son."

"Fuck what my momma misses! She might as well get over it because Jay Jay is dead. Ain't no going back. I am a transwoman. I am Jazmine now, and with all due respect because you just lost your son, I am going to let you know this one time and one time only, don't ever disrespect me about being who I am. I wouldn't speak at Robert's funeral now, even if he woke back up and asked me to," I yelled as I stormed off her porch.
I needed three bumps of coke after that shit.

I knew everyone wouldn't accept me as transwoman, but I guess since Robert was always my biggest supporter, I would have never imagined his funeral would be the first place I experienced transphobia. The day I went around my whole family as Jazmine during last Thanksgiving, my mom got drunk all day to hide the pain. She took it the worst, and to this day, I still don't understand why.

My grandmother and aunts were fine with it in my face, but I'm pretty sure they talked shit behind my back. At least they were supportive. My mom, on the other hand, wouldn't even speak to me. She says I ruined her life. Again, I am not sure how something I did with my body has ruined her life, but that's what she claims. My favorite little cousin, Ashley, was so excited to see me as a woman. She says I was so pretty, but then she asked what made me do it. What made me become a woman? The only response I could give her was that I was born a woman.

Jay Jay was always a vessel for Jazmine. He was born for me to grow into the person I would become. Jay Jay represents evolution and transformation. I am not different on the inside. The feelings and desires are the same as they were when I was considered a man. Just like being gay, nobody would choose a life of isolation or discrimination, but those are the things you are faced with when trying to live our truth.

Robert encouraged me to get my first plastic surgery last month, and I did. We were on the phone the whole time I was waiting to get under the knife to get my breasts done. I sent him pictures of the bandages and swelling while I was on bed rest at the hotel. He would send me pictures of his swollen feet. He was obsessed with those swollen feet. We were both recovering, so like I said, we talked a lot during his last days. I guess his recovery stopped, though. I still can't believe he's gone.

Eman

You know what one of my all-time favorite songs is that always gets me in my feelings? *Living All Alone* by Phyllis Hyman. Yeah, it's a sad song, but it was my momma's favorite. She used to play it all the time when I was younger. Phyllis was her favorite singer, and I know I am not old enough to be able to appreciate that kind of music, but her voice makes the hairs on the back of my neck stand up. Her voice is so full of richness and pain, and every note she sing embodies hurt. Right now, that's exactly how I feel. I'm hurting. My mom is gone, Robert gone, and I am scared as fuck about life in general.

I haven't shared this with Trayvon, but I think I'm battling depression. I've read different stuff about it, and it perfectly describes what I am going through. I barely want to get out the bed to do anything. I've been trying to be supportive for Tray and Jay Jay, but damn, I miss my momma! This shit doesn't ever seem to get any easier. Every little thing makes me miss her, and no matter how strong I pretend to be, I am weak.

I'm constantly reminded that I am truly in this world alone. I know I have my baby, and my friends, but I have no momma, and no daddy. I just feel empty. How do we little gay black boys make it through life like this, with no daddy? Yeah, shit happens, but not having a father is an epidemic in the gay life.

I've been laying across this bed for hours, trying to get enough strength to get dressed for this funeral, but I really don't want to go. I had nightmares all night, and I know I be scaring Trayvon, but I can't stop them. The nightmare always start off the same with my mommy talking to me, telling me to get my act together. As we're talking, it shifts into someone trying to murder her. Last night, the dream consisted of Robert sitting on her until she lost her breath. These dreams are horrible, and I decided not to tell Tray about last night's dream because it seemed in very bad taste to tell a dream about one dead person murdering another dead person.

The dreams are just bizarre all around. Jay Jay finally came home in the middle of the night without saying anything. I texted his ass about the plan to hit the road in a few days and get our asses to Atlanta, but he still hasn't responded back to me. I hope he's not getting cold feet because I need to move on, and get the hell out of Detroit. I'm tired of looking at these run-down houses and buildings. I want to see something better, something more alive. This city is depressing, and I just don't see a place here for me anymore.

"Are you ready," asks Trayvon

"Yeah, I am. Let's go. Thanks for ironing my clothes. Did you tell Jay Jay?"

"He already left. I went into his room, and it smelled like he smoked at least two blunts, and I saw empty coke bags all over his vanity. He's probably fucked up!"

"He probably is, knowing him."

Robert was definitely the mayor of the gays in this city. As soon as we pulled up, it felt like the fall out at the Post. Girls were standing all outside and around the church. I was a little disturbed about the look of his funeral. Everyone hugged and sent their condolences when they saw Tray and I because they knew how tight we are were. If you saw one of us, you knew the other three weren't far behind. I never had to go out and befriend many people because I had my friends that I enjoyed being around. We have had our ups and downs, but these last four years have been a blast with these motherfuckers. Now it's time to lay one of the Charmed Sisters to rest.

Once we walked into the sanctuary, I eventually saw Jay Jay. From what I could see of him, the bitch looked good. She was dressed in this black two-piece, pin-stripped blazer and skirt, with a bad ass long black wig that had a perfect part down the middle. She had some black frames that covered her eyes, and as I looked closer I think the bitch has gotten a boob job.

She made sure she came to this funeral looking like a million bucks for our friend, Robert. Tray and I sat in an open space on the third row, while Jay Jay sat in the second row with some of Robert's family. His funeral wasn't like my mom's at all. Hers was more family oriented, and felt a bit more homely. This funeral had a ton of people that weren't close to Robert, or his family. I knew most of the people there, but I was still shocked at some of the people that showed up.

I know Robert knew a lot of people, and during the time that we weren't speaking, he hung out of with other groups of friends from time to time, but he we always made it back to each other. His mom wasn't a simple lady, either. She had a service planned to put the Pope to rest.

The choir sang several gospel numbers. I knew most of them because Robert loved his gospel music. He would always act like he was a drag queen, and lip-synch to the Clark Sisters, especially Karen Clark. I broke down in tears when his aunts got up and sang *Endow Me*. It was so beautiful. Doctors from the hospital came and shared a few words from his last days at the hospital, and even his old boss shared some words.

The only people who spoke at my mom's funeral were me, and a few other family members. No outsiders were invited to speak. Robert's momma even had praise dancers come and perform in front of the church. This was truly a home going for Robert. It had his name written all over it. His mom and Jay Jay did a great job staying true to the kind of funeral that would have him smile from heaven.

After his mom finished the eulogy, and more people who were listed to speak stood up, I began waiting for Jay Jay to get up and say something. I was wondering why he wasn't listed anywhere on the program, considering I know he did most of the planning. He never stood up, though. Actually, I began looking at him from the row behind, and he was frozen. He was completely still. I started to get worried about him. I felt like we were not in synch with each other, and I needed him. I needed to talk to him, but for some reason, I couldn't get to him. It was like he was here, but he wasn't.

Eventually, they opened the floor for anyone who had any memories of Robert to come to the front, and share them with church. I knew my ass wasn't getting up, and I had so many memories to share about this motherfucker. I knew shit that would blow these people's minds, and as I begin to start laughing, thinking about the times Robert and I shared, I see Jay Jay, I mean Jazmine begin to walk to the mic.

"Hey, how are you guys doing out there?"
Silence pierced the room as everyone could see Jay Jay was intoxicated.

"I wasn't going to get up and say anything since I was politely asked not to speak at my best friend's funeral. Can you believe that shit? This lady right here told me because I have started transitioning into a woman, that she didn't want me to speak at her son's funeral. He was my best friend. He was the one who encouraged me to be whoever I wanted to be. He was the one who encouraged me to take the world by the balls and take ownership of that shit. Robert and I have been best friends since I was fourteen years old, and I'm being treated like an outsider because me becoming a woman didn't make his family comfortable. Robert bought me my first purse, my first pair of heels, and my first wig. He actually came up with the name Jazmine, and my new ID just came in the mail last week. Most of y'all are okay with the gays until y'all get a little uncomfortable. Y'all can use us for entertainment. We can do y'all hair. We can do your make-up. We can style your clothes, but when it's time for us to be our authentic selves, it's too much for y'all. Y'all motherfuckers don't have a clue what it's like to be black and gay around this bitch. It's hard for us. It was hard for Robert. Ms. Jones, you are like a second mother to me, and to know you think like this... it hurts. Maybe I just expected too much from you, maybe Robert expected too much for himself. I don't know, but all I got to say is that this is some bullshit. Look around at all the black gay people in here. Each one of us has a story to tell, and shit to get through."

"Jay Jay, shut up and sit your ass down! Why you got ruin this woman's son funeral?"

"You know what, momma, I was waiting on your old ass to get up and say something. I see you still can't take a real woman like myself. My fucking name is Jazmine, and I know for sure I'll see you in hell."

I immediately go and run to the stage after seeing him drop the mic, and fall to his knees. My friend needed me like never before, but instead of letting me embrace him and help him, he pushed me down to the ground, and runs out the church. The church begins getting loud from the people reacting to the drama that took place. Robert's mom gets in front of the church to calm everyone down. The gays started to leave church in a form of protest against the transphobia that Jay Jay made everyone aware of. His aunt begins arguing with another transwoman who began speaking loudly about her disgust with the family, and Tray jumped in between to intervene. This funeral turned into chaos. Damn you Robert, this one goes down in the history books!

Trayvon

Jay Jay is missing, and I don't know what the hell is going on. His phone is saying it's disconnected every time you call. His momma hasn't seen him since the funeral. I managed to find Michael's number from an old text message from Jay Jay, but when I call, it says his phone is disconnected, too. What the fuck is going on? Where is he?

He knows we are supposed to be hitting the road today, and nobody can find him. He was high at the funeral, and he just disappeared from the face of the earth. I know he took Robert's death harder than us, but there was no need to keep running to all of those damn drugs.

Who goes to a funeral high as a kite, and dressed like a slut from the eighties? Eman liked his outfit, but I thought it was a little inappropriate. Him showing all that fake cleavage was just too much. I know he is probably embarrassed about what happened at the funeral, but hell, it's over now. Time to move on; literally.

I'm guessing he went back to driving on the road, but it's not like him to not be available. He's always everybody's go to person. He is always available. Eman is barely reacting to the fact that Jay Jay is missing. He's acting like everything is okay, when I am freaking out.

Eman has been acting really weird lately. He's overly positive about every single thing. I know I shouldn't be complaining about that, but its strange to me, and his energy is on another level. It's borderline creepy. He barely talks, and when he does, its about winning in life, or exceeding in life goals. On top of that, he is now fully committed to Jesus, and this all happened in a week's time.

I know he's a new Christian, and he was recently baptized, but I'm not trying to date Donnie McClurklin . Maybe Kirk Franklin, but I can't do Donnie. He's just a little too much on the fake sanctified side for me. I've been catching him staring into space a lot lately, and it just looks like he has nothing in his eyes. I miss the dude I fell in love with, before all the deaths and drama.

I'm worried about him, but I decided to just let it play itself out. I know there is a lot going on, and maybe he will just shake out of whatever this mental stuff he is going through. I just hope he doesn't bring this baggage with us to Atlanta. I want a future with him, but the signs are scary. On the other hand, I love him, and I trust him. I truly believe he has my best interest at heart, so I will follow his lead and try not to question him.

Even though I am scared, it's interesting to watch him explores his life like this. I'm learning so much. It's like I have a set plan for my life, but with him, there's a freedom I wish I had. Just to be open for the world to be yours.

"I've loaded all of our stuff into the car," says Eman as he walks into the empty room where I was standing.

"Are you sure, Eman? I just don't feel comfortable leaving without Jay Jay, and leaving his stuff here."

"His mom is on top of this. She has the spare key. If he doesn't come back by the end of the month, she will have one of his cousins come over to move his stuff out. We packed most of it, so it wouldn't be that much they have to do."

"I know, but aren't you worried about him?"

"I'm not worried. I believe he's alright. He just doesn't want to be bothered. Maybe he wasn't ready to make such a huge move."

"Yeah, but what will you do for a roommate?"

"Well, I forgot to tell you something. My gay father left me some money for our trip to Atlanta. I have enough to cover Jay Jay's part for a couple of months, and then some. We are set!

"Eman, you know that money is illegal. It's been all on the news. I thought you told me you weren't involved in the money side with the House of Dollars?"

"Baby, I asked my gay daddy, and he says it legit. It's untraceable. We good, I promise."

"I know him, and that house you're in, and they don't have a history of being honest. They are thieves and crooks. Baby, you gotta be sure it's okay for you to take that money. I don't want you getting caught up in all that.

"It's too late. I've already bought money orders and paid my rent up for the year."

"Eman, if you think it's fine, then I ain't gone trip. I'm just glad you have somewhere to stay."

"Yeah, we gone live so close to each other. Me and you, Tray."

"Wow! That's good, but why are you so quick to act like Jay Jay is not coming to Atlanta, too. He might be down there already, and you making all these plans without him."

"You're right, he might be. We might get down there, and he'll already be moved in, with a new number, and living the life. Or, he might not be. He might never move, and I'll be stuck looking dumb, waiting on him and suffering. I gotta be prepared. I'm tired of suffering. I need a break, baby."

"Yeah, you're right. He is older than both of us, so I figure he knows what he's doing. I just wished I knew he was okay, and maybe that would ease my mind. He was just so messed up the last time we saw him."

"You're right. He could at least let us know he's okay. Anything really could happen on those back roads, not to mention Michael's crazy ass. Ain't no telling what he's capable of if Jay Jay pushes him too far."

"Please, don't put that thought into my head."

"I'm just saying, Jay Jay will be fine, he has the Lord on his side."

"Will you please stop with all this God stuff? I'm serious! I am worried about him."

"I'm worried, too, but I am also worried you're going to be late for your first day of classes."

"I know. We have to leave now."

"Let's go then, baby. We can talk in the car. We got to hit the road."

As I got into the car knowing I was leaving Detroit to go to college, I was hit with adrenaline. I started to think about my momma, GeGe, and how I said my good byes to them the day before. I thought of my city, Detroit. The place that made me, and spared nothing. It gave me all that it had; the good, bad, and the ugly. Most of all, I thought about the Ya Ya sisterhood, and what it had become. We were just four friends living life, not knowing what path was in our future, but we certainly lived in the moment.

We relied on each other to provide things our actual families weren't able to. We understood each other, even when it seemed like we had to survive warfare. Because of Robert, Jay Jay, and Eman, I am much stronger. They built me up to be able to handle things, and they gave me love like no other. Ain't nothing like having a friendship that carried you across deep waters and hurricane. Robert is gone, may God bless his soul. He left way too soon. Jay Jay, aka Jazmine, was the glue to the sisterhood. I hope she returns to start this new journey. I want my sister. And Eman; ain't no telling where this is going, but for now, I'm good. Having your man as your best friend is more than enough.

"Baby, what you over there thinking about?"

"Oh, nothing. Do we take I-75 all the way there?"

"Yeah, its a straight shot to ATL."

"Cool. Do you think our relationship can handle all these gays down there?"

"Hell, it better! You are mine, as long as you don't forget that, baby. Besides, we are young. We'll figure it out. I'm pretty sure we will do what's best for us."

"That's true."

"You excited?"

"Yeah, I am. I'm actually really excited."

Acknowledgments

First of all, I have to give thanks to the most high for protection, guidance, and grace. Thanks to my mother for always loving and encouraging me, to my sisters Tenee, and Nea, my grandmother, and all of my family and friends for their unconditional love and support.

To my best friend, Eric, I give you much praise for being my rock. You have always been the person I could rely and depend on. We have been on this journey from the very beginning, and I get so much joy knowing that this is only the beginning for us. To my brothers, Darnell and Tyrone, thanks for showing me what true friendship means, no matter where on earth we are.

Thanks to all my tribes and communities that have helped mold and shape me into the man I am today. My hometown of Detroit, Bowling Green State University, Atlanta, Austin, Ballroom, and Theater.

I am grateful to all of those with whom I have had the pleasure to work with during this project including Parkco, Jacob, Franco, and Warren. To everyone who has supported any of my plays, readings, or community events, I am forever thankful for the love and support. Thank you for being apart of the dream, vision, and the mission. Without you, I can't do the work.

To my idol, James Baldwin, your work allowed this little black queer boy to believe and dream that I could use my words to impact the world. Because of you, I will continue to tell the stories that need to be told.